My Fake Holiday Love

CD Giles

Print ISBN: 979-8-9859305-4-2

eBook ISBN: 979-8-9859305-5-9

First Edition

Acknowledgements

I have to start by thanking my hubby. If it wasn't for you showing me that happily ever after does exist, I would have never had the inspiration to write. I love you babe. Thanks for always believing in me and giving me the confidence to believe that my dreams can come true.

To my ray of sunshine, thank you for being in this journey with me. You helped me in more ways than I can count. Love you to the moon and back.

To my family, thank you for your love and dedication throughout the years. I have some strong role models who have helped me navigate this world. You give me strength with your love that fuels me. I love you with all my heart.

My girl tribe – what can I say – you have been my rock throughout the years. I know that I can call at any hour of the day and you'll be there. Thank you for helping me harness my girl power. Love you to pieces.

Chapter One

Jacqui

"Hey Jae, are you sure you don't need me to do anything else for the baby shower tomorrow?" My twin brother, Jake, asks as he walks into my office with a smile so bright, like a cloudless, sunny Texas day.

My smile mirrors Jake's as I stand and walk around my desk. He's been over the moon since he and Gabi found out that not only are they having a baby, but they're having twin girls. Pink explosions at tomorrow's baby shower will be everywhere, from the cake to the decorations. I'm surprised Jake doesn't find an excuse to stay far, far away.

Jake and Gabi met on a seven-day cruise a year and a half ago. Jake told me he fell in love the moment he laid eyes on her. Determined to convince Gabi that their time together on the cruise wasn't a fling, he proved he was a man of his word. Not letting distance, their different backgrounds or race come between them, he slayed her dragons. They married six months later. Jake confided with me he and Gabi planned to secretly eloped a few times. With this being the first wedding on both sides for the families, they didn't want to disappoint anyone, especially the moms who demanded they needed time to plan the wedding.

"Between mom and Gabi's mom, I've only had to coordinate the cake, gift table, and the backdrop for the photos. We're good. Just make sure you bring the muscle. Your living room furniture needs to be rearranged to accommodate everything."

Jake leans against my credenza with his arms crossed. "Don't worry, I spoke to Travis and CJ earlier today. They both confirmed to be at my house at eleven o'clock sharp."

I smirked. We both know that Travis never arrives on time for a-n-y-t-h-i-n-g except for training for his precious triathlons. "Are you sure about Travis?"

"I've warned him if he's not there to set up, he's on cleanup duty."

"Well, are you sure that his majesty knows how to do manual labor?"

"Jae, not sure why you're so hard on Travis. He's actually a hardworking and pretty well-rounded guy."

I mumble, *how would I know* so low that Jake doesn't hear me. He leans closer and asks, "What did you say?"

"I said 'hope that he shows'–enough about Travis. How's Gabi feeling these days? I haven't seen her in a few weeks."

"She's fine and gets more beautiful with each passing day. I never understood the saying 'pregnant women glow,' but I get it now. Gabi looks radiant and the girls grow more and more every day. I'm going on record that I'm not the one saying this, but Gabi keeps complaining she feels like a beached whale. All I see is the woman I'm head over heels in love with–swollen ankles and all."

While acting like I'm gagging, I roll my eyes, then laugh and give him a gushy sister hug. "I'm so happy for y'all. I still can't believe that I'm not only going to be an aunt, but I'm going to be a twin aunt. None of my friends have this bragging right. I'm warning you now that I'm spoiling the girls. Have y'all decided on names yet?"

"The list remains pretty long, but we have knocked a few names off the list. Gabi's method includes whether she knows someone with the name—if she does, she assesses whether she likes their disposition. Any red flags—off the list they go. After we shorten the list to our top ten, the girls will help us with the final name selections. We want names that fit them."

"Love y'all's approach—now scoot. My boss is a hard ass and demands I have this first design before I leave the office today."

"Funny Jae. I may just tell dad you called him a hard ass."

I playfully throw a wadded piece of paper at him. "See you tomorrow. Let me know if you need anything else for the baby shower."

Jake and Gabi's huge, Mediterranean-style first floor open concept looks transformed with the 'It's Twins' photo backdrop commanding the room with pink, fuchsia, and gold balloons arranged in several intricate balloon towers. Secretly, this is my favorite display, even though the gift tables come in a close second.

Both moms titter here and there, working on every detail. Instead of losing my twin after he married the love of his life, I gained Gabi's mom. I could only call Gabi's mom Momma G, no matter how hard I tried to call her Mrs. St. Clair or Ms. Gisselle.

Just as I turn to head back to the babies' gift table, Gabi waddles into the room, her hands cradling her rounded belly as she moves with a gentle sway. "How's my favorite sister? Are my nieces treating you well?"

"Jae, I'm moving slow today. Jake had to help me get ready and..."

But I don't let Gabi finish. I jump into full panic mode. "Are you having contractions right now? I didn't want to say anything, but it looks like you've dropped some. Do I need to go find Jake?"

Gabi places her hand on my arm. "Jae, whoa... you're as bad as Jake. He's as nervous as a turkey the week before Thanksgiving. I'm fine.

Your nieces are very active right now and my lower back is killing me something fierce."

My anxiety remains high, but I try to relax for Gabi's sake. In the voice that Jake named 'my teacher calm voice' back when we interned for dad our sophomore year of college, I ask. "Do you want to sit down?"

"Jae, if you don't stop, Jake will think something is wrong and I don't need him hovering any more than he already is. Do you know he refuses to take any more business trips until after the girls are born and works from home most days? I still have six weeks before the girls are due to arrive."

Gabi stops her tirade to look around. She looks happy but I notice her eyes well with tears, "Oh no, Gabi... what's wrong? Why are you crying?"

"I'm fine... remember, I have double the dose of pregnancy hormones." Gabi looks around then says, "Everything looks beautiful. I love what you did with the gift table and the photo backdrop. When will the photographer be here?"

"She'll be here in about fifteen minutes... she texted to let me know she was exiting the Beltway. Do you want to sit while you wait?"

"You've already asked me if I want to sit down. The stubborn side of me wants to say no, but I'm already tired just from walking down the hall from the bedroom."

The baby shower ended half an hour ago and almost everyone has gone home. We played the usual baby shower games. Just going on record that the 'guess what's in the diaper' game was absolutely disgusting. Even my competitive side didn't surface—I couldn't force myself to try to win.

I just need a moment to myself, so I escaped to the wine cellar. The baby shower has been equal parts fun and hard work. The breakup with my ex-fiancé, Jeremy, six months ago, eclipses my elation today at becoming an aunt. Today would have been our three-month anniversary. Cutting into my reflection, my phone dings. I open the Instagram notification more from muscle memory and see a repost by someone I follow because we used to run in the same circles. Why did I have to see this and now of all times? A smiling Jeremy and the girl that I caught him having sex in our bed stares at me. The cherry on top, the caption reads, '*She said Yes.*'

I don't believe this shit. This asshat got engaged and I haven't even been able to date. The wine cellar, positioned down a long hallway and down a set of stairs on the other side of the house, gives me the privacy I need. Something breaks within me and I cry like I lost my best friend.

Not sure how long I've been down here, but I hear the voice of the last person I want to see me like this. "Jae, hey… hey, look at me," says Travis with so much concern and tenderness that I freeze.

He gently turns me around and takes two fingers to lift my chin until my down-turned eyes look at him. I'm a mess. God only knows how I look right now.

"Please leave," I beg Travis. My voice sounds water-logged even to my ears. Travis has never been one to take orders, probably from all the heated-verbal volleyball matches that he's had over the years with his dad.

Travis searches my face, looking for answers I'd rather remain buried. "I'm not going anywhere, Jae, until you tell me what's wrong."

As I bury my face in the crook of his neck, I mumble, "Nothing." Two things I recognize at once… he smells scrumptious like a woodsy, smoky scent and his chest feels like a solid wall of muscles as his arms band around me. This hug makes me wish I found an excuse sooner to hug Travis instead of now, in my brother's wine cellar. Travis could open a pop-up store and charge for these hugs. Hands down, I'd be waiting in line.

Sucks having to put my life back together at thirty-five after finding my cheating fiancé in bed with his NOW fiancée. Thinking of the life that I thought I would have by now, a husband and maybe carrying our first child, makes me burst into heart-wrenching sobs. I don't have the strength to stop. Travis holds me tighter as he lets me cry until I have nothing left.

Travis

I'm not sure why I followed Jacqui. She seemed off today, so I wanted to make sure that she was okay. Why she's so upset baffles me, but I refuse to leave her alone to deal with this by herself.

"Do you want to talk about it? You and I were close once. Remember, in ninth grade, when Russell ruined your final art project? Jake and I switched Russell's test with John's. John got the ninety-five and Russell, well... he got what he deserved."

This makes Jacqui laugh a little. Good, anything is better than standing here not knowing what to do while she cries her heart out.

Jae steps back as she tries to collect herself. An internal debate must war within Jae because she takes a while to speak. "Travis, really, let me just get myself together, then I promise to head back to help clean up."

My resolve strengthens. Jae needs to understand I am as stubborn as she is. Nothing could make me leave her alone. The options become clear. My best approach, assure Jae, nothing needs to be done. "Jae, we did everything except for the photo backdrop. Gabi asked us to leave it so she and Jake can take more photos with the photographer tomorrow. No need to rush back. Actually, you can leave through the side door if you'd rather head straight home. I don't mind running interference with Jake. I can tell him I saw you leave."

"Why would you do that, Travis? We don't even talk to each other."

I take my hand and rub the back of my neck while trying to form a logical explanation. What would Jacqui do if she knew I've wanted her since the eleventh grade? For eighteen long years! She would think I was pathetic. With her wrapped in my arms a few moments ago, I am having a hard time thinking. She was right when she said we barely speak, but not because I haven't wanted to.

"Ok, Jae, enough stalling... what's going on?"

She lets out an enormous sigh, like the weight of the world rests on her shoulders. With more patience than I normally have, I wait while she decides whether she's going to tell me. Pretty sure that she'd rather tell anyone but me. I'm just her brother's annoying best friend.

What I wouldn't do for her to see me as more, as the man that's adored her for what feels like forever. I blame myself if she sees me as a womanizing man with more one-night stands than I care to count. Would she find humor if she knew I only started down this path because the one girl that I wanted was off limits?

I knew Jake would have my hide if I tried to hook up with his baby sister. Technically, they have the same birthday, but she arrived four-minutes later. Jake takes his big-brother responsibilities seriously.

The bar towels stored next to the wine glasses catch my attention; I hand a towel to Jae, watch as she wipes her face and takes another gigantic sigh to fortify herself. "I'm just going to rip off the band aid. My ex-fiancé got engaged today. The repost of the photo with the caption 'she said yes' brought back the hurt and humiliation. I thought I had moved on, but apparently not. Today would have been of our three-month wedding anniversary." Jacqui sniffs and angrily wipes as a few large tears drop on her cheek.

I clench my fists, trying to stop the urge to find that asshole, and beat his face in. "Well, I know my opinion doesn't count, but I never liked Jeremy and I'll go further to say I always questioned his intentions." I pause because I don't think this is what she wants or needs to hear. I change tactics and go with what's in my heart. "You're beautiful, Jae. You deserve so much more. Someone who loves you unconditionally and knows without a doubt no one on this earth comes close to you."

I want to kiss her so badly right now as my eyes rake over every aspect of Jae, her tempting, kissable lips, her slim waist and rounded hips. Hips perfect for my hands to grip. I'm so close to pulling her in for a kiss, I force myself to take a small step back.

Jacqui looks at me, blinking as if she sees me for the first time. I probably revealed too much, but I really don't care right now. Jae is the priority. I don't want her wasting another tear on that loser.

Before I'm aware of what's happening, I feel Jae step into me. She licks my lower lip with her tongue. I open for her but keep the kiss light, letting her set the pace. I feel chills trail down my spine as I try to hold back.

Jae tightens her arms around my neck and whispers against my lips, "Travis, kiss me like I mean something to you."

This woman brings me to my knees. I groan as I pull her tight against me. I drop my head and claim her mouth in a searing kiss that lets her know that I'm a man who knows exactly who he's kissing.

A door nearby slams shut, causing Jae and I to jump apart.

Jacqui's eyes face the floor as she says, "Thanks Travis. I just needed to feel, even if for a few minutes, that I... I..." The pale skin on her neck is flushed red as she looked everywhere but at me.

My first instinct finds me reaching for Jae as she turns to walk away. If I could keep her here a little longer, maybe I could show her she's better off without Jeremy. I want to say more, but all I manage is, "My pleasure."

Man, when did I look at Jae as anything but Jake's annoying little sister? Unfortunately, I know the answer to this question. It was the summer when she turned seventeen. Jae was a late bloomer, but my God did he save the best for last.

I'll never forget when she walked into the backyard wearing a bright orange bikini showing off legs for days and her breasts. They weren't spilling out of her bikini top, but they might as well have been because I imagined her well defined D cups spilling out in my hands. This walk down memory lane proves to be painful—I'm getting hard—especially after having Jacqui and her curves in my hands. I forced myself to think of intellectual property law, my grandma's dentures, and the poop diapers Jake will change soon—that did the trick.

After taking a fortifying deep breath, I try to settle the pent-up energy. Sad reality, only one woman can assuage my need. With my head bent down, I head back to the great room to check if Jake needs anything. Once home, I'll try to wrap my head around what the hell just happened.

Chapter Two

Travis

Our trio triathlon training group is now down to a duo. Jake refuses to leave Gabi's side with only six weeks to D Day, leaving CJ and me to our 40-minute run around the Rice University campus. We wanted to avoid the Sunday crowds, so we opted for Rice in hopes students had gone home for Thanksgiving.

My thoughts go to Jacqui yesterday, but not the crying spell. Oh, no, I want her back in my arms. How would I even broach the subject? Would Jae believe I haven't been with anyone since Jake shared her wedding was off? Knowing she was back on the market makes me want to take my shot; let her know I want to date her; and see if she can see me as a man... her man. The biggest hurdle... Jake, my best friend. Not even sure what Jake would do if he knew I want to explore a relationship with Jae.

Even knowing this, looking into Jacqui's deep blue eyes yesterday made me want to be the guy who puts the laughter and sparkle back. The ocean of emotions in her eyes took me under the surface. I would have happily drowned in her depths. Even puffy eyed, she remains the most beautiful woman in my world... the one who got away. Her five-foot six height fits perfectly with my six foot three.

We just fit. I realized how right she felt in my arms when she cried in the crook of my neck. Her light brown hair with blond highlights felt like silk against my skin. I exhale. What am I going to do?

We turn onto Main Street before CJ asks, "What's up, man? You're not usually this quiet."

"Work stuff." I change the subject before CJ inquires. CJ could easily be a lawyer. His cross-examination skills exceed some of my junior attorneys. "Never been to a baby shower before, glad that Jake thought about having our favorite bar food and beer in his man cave for us. I started having hives being around all that pink."

"Yeah, using us for the muscle gave us something productive to do. Bonus... it gave me an opportunity to see Samantha."

"I noticed you checking her out, and this isn't the first time, mind you. What's holding you back? Are you going to ask her out?" My smile forms as I give CJ shit. We all know how much he likes Sam.

"My plan is to use strategy and finesse the shit out of my approach. I'm waiting for Sam to tire of dating the trail of losers."

"Well, don't wait too long. You know what they say 'you snooze, you lose.'"

"Don't worry about me. I could say the same thing about you."

"What are you talking about, CJ?"

"Don't think that I haven't noticed your hiatus. Everything ok?"

I want to confide in CJ... I really do, but confiding with him would place him in a position where eventually he would need to keep my secret from Jake. Best to stick with my work excuse. "Work is busy right now with our latest acquisition. This deal contains five patents with two more patents pending and a federal six-month review before the deal can close. My role as the lead intellectual property attorney keeps me working long hours, besides leading a team of five junior attorneys. Nothing else is going on... only work."

Talk about the understatement of the year... getting a taste of Jacqui opened a pandora's box for me, wanting to explore her in every way. As my fitness watch buzzes with an incoming notification, I glance at the screen. Unknown number. My heart races as I realize it's from Jacqui. I take a deep breath, my mind racing with questions about what she could want. My fingers tremble slightly as I open the message, trying to hide the nervousness that's settled in the pit of my stomach. Now, I'm really distracted. This run can't be over fast enough.

Jacqui

My sun-filled backroom brings me joy. This space allows me to pursue my first love—painting. The contemporary piece commissioned for the New York Renaissance Women's exhibit for next weekend is my first public exhibit. Asked to take part two months ago by a friend from my days at NYU, both energized and scared me to no end. Now, I'm glad that I said yes as I stand back and examine my work. This piece reflects my range of emotions over the past six months... sadness, acquiescence, driven, and hurt.

Jake knows I paint when I'm stressed, and my mom thinks painting is just a hobby. How do I share with her and dad that I don't want to work at the architectural firm my grandfather founded anymore? Painting calls me... fuels me. When I paint, I feel energized. Jeremy's infidelity drove me back to painting.

Before I called off the wedding, my Type-A, supercharged wedding planning took over my life. I wanted everything to be perfect, every detail covered in my wedding planning spreadsheet. Work, wedding planning, exercise, and dieting took up all my time, leaving none for

Jeremy. Focused on fitting into a size two wedding dress, when I normally wear a size six, took over every aspect of my life.

After catching Jeremy with that girl, I blamed myself at first. I should have spent more time with him... I should have hired a wedding planner like he recommended. I shoulda, woulda, coulda'd myself past delirium. When Gabi asked me if I was happy with Jeremy, I couldn't remember any moments of genuine joy. If I compared how I felt with Jeremy and how I feel when I'm painting, there is no comparison. When I paint, I feel as if I'm lit from the inside. I always want one more... one more minute, one more paint stroke, one more image on the canvas.

Jeremy attended the MD Anderson gala my mom chairs almost two years ago. Enamored with Jeremy's celebrity and political connections, I never took the time to look past the façade. After a whirlwind courtship, Jeremy asked me to marry him six months to the day that we met. As I look back, I said 'yes' for so many reasons, not all of them good. He ticked off a lot of boxes on my list... financially stable—check; actively takes part in causes important to him—check; likes kids—check; good in bed–no, no, that wasn't a check; I got used to mediocre sex. I told myself it would get better in time.

Sadly, I said 'yes' more because all of my girlfriends were already married and starting a family or engaged and soon-to-be married. None are good reasons.

My gasp takes me by surprise as an epiphany forms... I'm hurt and embarrassed, but not heartbroken. In order to be heartbroken, my heart had to be involved, which it wasn't. I thought I would grow to love Jeremy because of the common background we have. Who wouldn't want to live in an affluent gated community and have kids who attend preschools with long waiting lists? Or join an exclusive country club and become a woman with a calendar filled with charity work?

After my kiss last night with Travis, the kiss that rocked my world, I barely missed being in a loveless marriage with a man that I really didn't like. He was pompous on a good day and arrogant, thinking that he was the smartest person in the room on the other days. How did I not see this before?

No, the kiss that I initiated with Travis proved chemistry exists. Who would have known the chemistry would be with a man who has known me since I had braces? When he kissed me back, wow! No one has ever kissed me like he needed to kiss me more than he wanted to take his next breath. Once I got home, I needed Alex, my electronic boyfriend, for a much-needed release after that kiss.

Unconsciously, I press my legs together, remembering Travis's tight grip as he held me. He became my anchor as I broke down. Later, I recalled the definition of his muscular chest and thighs. When I wore heels, Jeremy and I were the same height. Travis though... he towered over me at six foot three with wavy brown hair that I wanted to run my hands through. I felt protected and cherished as I fell apart. Man, his eyes—when my eyes locked with his grayish blue eyes, I saw genuine concern and something else that I couldn't quite pinpoint.

A bone-tired sigh escapes my lips as my doorbell rings. I look down at the image from my video doorbell, then notice my paint splattered shirt. Travis arrived faster than I thought. Now, I'm worried that I should have put on a little makeup, maybe fixed my hair or at least changed into a clean t-shirt with yoga pants.

As I walk to the door, I take a fortifying breath to garner the strength I will need to ask Travis for a monumental favor. Well, here goes nothing. I open the door. Seeing Travis in all his six-three yumminess makes my mouth water. The well-worn jeans capture my attention, but I look away before my eyes travel lower. No, it's much safer to look higher. The fitted long sleeve light blue t-shirt pulls tight over his muscles. What I wouldn't do to kiss him again… of course, it would be for purely scientific reasons to see if the chemistry thing was a fluke. His eyes seize my full attention as I fight for control. His ego is already big enough… no need to become just another female who thinks Travis Prescott invented orgasms. Hopefully, Travis didn't catch me checking him out. I need to remain cool and collected. I step aside and tell Travis, "Come in."

As covert as possible, I watch as Travis admires my décor. "Wow, Jae, I like how you decorated."

His reaction fills me with pride. Girlfriends gush about my interior design skills when they visit. The dark blue center contrast wall against the light tan walls compliments the light gray sectional with off-white and blue pillows. Teakwood accessories add the modern touches that I wanted. "Glad you like it. I've taken my time to only purchase items I love."

He continues to scan the room while nodding appreciatively. "Well, you've done a fantastic job. I haven't been here since your first month here when I helped Jake carry the chair that you found at that estate sale in Montrose. Where did you end up putting it?"

"I put it in my sunroom in the back. I like to relax and drink coffee while the sun rises."

"Sunrise? Are you still an early riser, getting up before six in the morning?"

To deflect the awkwardness trying to settle over us like a gray cloud, I casually walk towards the kitchen. "Old habits, what can I say? Would you like anything to drink? I keep the beer that you and Jake like ice cold."

"Sure." Travis coughs, then starts. "Hey, Jae… about yesterday…"

While giving Travis a beer and pouring me some wine, I interrupt him. "Travis, we're good. I know what you're going to say, but I called you over for a different reason."

Travis's eyebrows crease in confusion as his eyes focus on me with disbelief. "Yeah?"

"I need... I'm not sure how to put it, so I'm just going to say it. I need you to pretend to be my boyfriend, at least until New Year's."

Travis is about to interrupt but I continue, "Let me finish before you shoot this idea down. I need to go to New York next weekend for an art event on Friday evening where I'd prefer not to go solo. Then my friend Brittney asked me to be her maid of honor for her New Year's Eve wedding. I responded with a plus one for the wedding, thinking I would surely have someone that I could take by the time of the wedding. Well, I've tried to get back on the proverbial dating horse, but let's just say that it's been harder than I thought it would be."

Travis

When Jacqui opened the door, I stood frozen, unable to move like ice blocks encased my feet. Jae wore a paint-splattered top with loose pants to match. None of these matters. Her beauty still captured me, making me want to grab and kiss her senseless. It took me a moment to regain my composure and walk inside.

Prepared for practically anything except her request. Pretend to be Jae's boyfriend?

A million thoughts run through my mind right now... this could be my chance to show Jacqui how I feel about her; I really want another opportunity to have her in my arms. The feel of her body pressed up against mine kept me up last night... I woke harder than I have ever been. Only after taking matters in my hand, could I get dressed for my run with CJ. Last but not least, what would Jake do if he found out? If I had a sister, I wouldn't want her to date a man with my track record. "I don't know Jae. What about Jake?"

"I'm not worried about Jake, besides Jake is pre-occupied. With Gabi only six weeks away from having the twins. Jake doesn't leave her side, hovering like a mother hen."

The bark of laughter erupts from deep within. "A mother hen. What I wouldn't do to tell him you called him a mother hen!" I pause before continuing, "You're asking me to cross a line with my best friend. I don't know Jae." As an only child, Jake became the brother that I never had and their dad... well, he's the father that I wished I had. I... I just don't know.

"Jake won't find out. I only need you for the next five weeks. Then we go back to how we are with each other, barely saying hello, let alone speaking to each other. Travis, I don't mean this in a bad way, but we both know that you're not my type. I wouldn't ask if I wasn't desperate."

Her words punched me in the gut, but I give a wry chuckle, trying to act if her words weren't a direct hit. "Yeah, you're doing wonders for my self-esteem here. I really need to think this through. If I say yes, I take it we'll need to leave Friday morning? The day after Thanksgiving, I might add—so you're there in time for the art event. Is that correct?"

"I get that I'm infringing on your personal life. Oh my God, I didn't even think. Are you currently dating anyone?"

The shocked look on Jae's face reminds me of the girl I first met back in high school. A memory flashes of Jae with braces. Man, this could go badly for me. The potential loss of my relationship with Jake and his parents tops the list on why I should tell Jae '*No*' now and run while I have a chance.

"No, Jae, I'm not dating anyone, and I don't have any plans this weekend." Jae brightens at this admission. I hate to burst her bubble, but

I add, "This is a big ask. I need time to really think this through. Can I get back with you by tomorrow night?"

"Travis, your mom is holding on line one. She's already called twice this morning and says she'll hold until you pick up. What do you want me to tell her?"

"I'll take the call. Sabrina, give me a minute to walk to my office." After I hang up with my executive assistant, I need to give her something extra special this holiday for having to deal with my mother all year. Mom's behavior continues to get progressively worse. Probably attributed to my dad's open affair with a girl in her twenties, supposedly meeting her at a speaking engagement earlier this year. Decorum is no longer a driving factor—my dad spends most nights in his downtown penthouse condo with said girlfriend while my mom stays in my eight-bedroom childhood estate.

The fortifying breath I take doesn't help reduce my frustration. Now is not the time for my mom's irrational behavior. Losing two work days because of the Thanksgiving holiday, my team and I plan to stay late for the next three days. Not caring if my impatience shows in my voice, I close my door and pick up the call. "Hi, mother, everything ok?"

"No, Travis, everything isn't okay. Your father brought his whore to our country club for brunch yesterday. Julie couldn't wait to share that little piece of news with me."

I count to three before answering. "You haven't even blinked an eye before and you have your own companion, Arnold. Why does this even bother you now?"

She sputters as she answers, "Arnold... Arnold and I are discreet, that's the difference. Arnold doesn't spend a night. You need to take my side, Travis. Your dad continues to make a mockery of our family."

Family... the words I really want to say I refrain from saying in deference to my mom. "I don't think what we have meets the definition of a family. Mom, is there anything else? You interrupted a strategy session that I need to get back to."

My mom tries another tactic and changes the tone of her voice. The righteous outrage gone and replaced with a sugary Southern tone. "Travis, I wish you had time for your mother. I wish things were different between us."

Never having a problem with allowing the parade of nannies to raise me, she couldn't bother with even trying to deal with a toddler, let alone a teenager. Yeah, I wish things were different as well, but I don't have the time to deal with her right now. I huff and try to remove the irritation from my voice. "Was there anything else, mother?"

"Yes, do you plan to have Thanksgiving dinner with your dad and me?"

Dropping my head and pinching the bridge of my nose, why would she even think that I'd sit down for that shit show? Not even sure why they're keeping this charade. "Mother, I can't make any promises, but will try to swing by. I really have to go."

Not my proudest moment, I hang up to my mom saying, "Travis Colton Prescott I am not..."

My corner office oversees downtown Houston. This view affirms all the late nights and weekends were worth it. I notice the darkness, then look at my watch... damn, how can it already be after seven o'clock?

Where did the time go? After the strategy session, I began writing exhibits for the purchase sale agreement. Better call Jae. Even though she may not realize it yet, I'm a man of a word.

My internal deliberation on whether to go along with Jae's proposal volleyed back and forth all day between *hell no* and *let's see how this weekend goes*. Any time I considered Jake, the answer became a firm hell no. But I couldn't get the image of Jacqui crying in my arms after the baby shower to escape my memory. Not being there for Jae over the years pushed the decision in her favor.

Jacqui picks up after the second ring. "Hey Jae, apologies for taking all day to call you." I pause before continuing, "I'm going on the record that this is a bad idea. The only reason that I'm halfway considering this is if we establish some ground rules."

Jacqui's excited voice comes through the phone. "Of course. Where do you want to start?"

"How do you see us doing this?" I ask in a frustrated grumble.

"Well, when we're in Houston, we can act like we normally do. I barely acknowledge you and vice versa."

I chuckle, "Ok, got it. Continue to act normal. When we travel, I don't mind getting a separate room."

Jae pauses and sighs. "I thought we should probably get a suite with two separate rooms. Some members of the wedding party are staying at the hotel where I plan to stay next weekend. To be on the safe side, we should get one room."

Frustrated, I pace. My ache for Jacqui pulsates, gaining intensity. No matter what I do, going back to how I was with Jae before the kiss seems like an unsurmountable feat. Truthfully, getting separate rooms was my best defense for surviving this weekend. "Ok, you have a good point, but we have a problem. We really don't know each other."

"You're right. I was thinking about this as well. On our flight to New York, we can walk through the basics, so our relationship looks legit."

Surprised I didn't think of that... My only defense, throughout the day I drove myself delirious vacillating between saying '*yes*' to Jae's proposition and saying '*no, what the hell are you thinking*'. "That's actually an excellent use of our three plus hours together."

In a serious tone, Jae continues, "Ok, so we agree. Next, you can't tell CJ, especially not Jake. He can't find out."

My bark of laughter reverberates throughout my office. Does she think I have a death wish? No problems with me abiding by this edict. "I'd like to see my thirty-sixth birthday. You get no arguments from me. This stays between us. Anything else?"

Jacqui pauses and clears her throat. "We have to be exclusive while we have this pretend relationship."

In a serious voice, while crossing my arms over my chest, I express. "That may be a deal breaker for me."

Jacqui sputters. "Tra... Travis"

I can't keep up the farce. The shocked look I imagine on Jae's face makes me burst out laughing. "I'm kidding... I'm kidding. Being exclusive won't be a problem." I can hear her breathy exhale through the phone, and it sends an ache straight to my dick, only confirming... this is a bad idea.

"Good. Ok, well, I'll send you the logistics for the flight and itinerary for this weekend. Oh, before I forget Friday evening, you'll need to wear one of those fancy suits of yours."

"Got it. If you think of anything else, just let me know."

Chapter Three

Jacqui

Excited Travis said yes to this fake relationship helped me to relax and look forward to the holidays. Thanksgiving hands down is my favorite holiday. I love catching up with family and eating my favorite foods that my mom only cooks once a year.

My mom's car sits near the side entrance to the house underneath the covered car pad... dad must still be at the office.

Mom and Dad moved into this Italian-inspired house when Jake and I turned four. Before middle school, I didn't realize that we lived in the prestigious Boulevard Oaks historic district. This was just the neighborhood where I played with my friends. The two-story eight thousand square foot house always seemed majestic, like living in my own Italian castle.

Dad took mom to Italy for their honeymoon where mom fell in love with the architecture. Dad loves to the tell the story how he found this house. After leaving an architectural society meeting, dad drove through Boulevard Oaks where he stumbled upon this house. The house wasn't for sale but my dad stopped and talked to the owner, asking that he let him know if he was ever in the market to sell.

Two short years later, the family needed to sell to move to Seattle. My dad paid the asking price and move us in a month before Thanksgiving, to my mom's delight. The gigantic kitchen provides the perfect backdrop for the parties that my parents love to throw.

"Hey mom," I call out while taking off my light coat and gloves as I look up at the beautiful hand painted frescos in the ceiling (my idea). After studying Italian art, I became obsessed and told my mom that it was ridiculous to live in an Italian styled home and not have any painted ceilings. To my thirteen-year-old brain, my logic sounded solid. My mom found an Italian painter who had moved with his family to Houston.

Pots clang down the hall, so I follow the sound and see my mom in her recently upgraded kitchen with a large island bar in the middle and stainless-steel appliances. Hands down, I covet the navy-blue Viking stove with a double oven. One day, I plan to have the turquoise color. I bend and kiss my mom on the cheek. "Mom, everything smells delicious. I see dad got you to make his favorite red mashed potatoes."

My mom wipes her hands on her apron while turning with a big smile on her face. "Hi, sweetheart. What a pleasant surprise. Didn't expect to see you until tomorrow."

"Well, I thought I would come over tonight and help with anything that you need. I brought my clothes to spend the night. Before I forget, you remember that I have to be in New York this weekend?"

"Yes, I remember you mentioning that you'd be in New York for your friend's bridal shower. How are the fittings going?"

"Good, we have our last fitting Saturday morning before the shower in the afternoon. Brittney even chose bridesmaids' dresses that I actually like. Not saying that, I'll find another opportunity to wear the dress, but it's not out of the realm of possibility."

"Tell Brittney we send our love." My mom slaps her hand lightly on her forehead, "Oh my goodness, with everything going on with Jake and Gabi, I haven't bought Brittney a wedding present yet."

"Don't worry. You still have time. I'll do some intel this weekend to see what's still on her registry that she really wants, then I'll get it for you."

"Oh Jacqui, that would be great. I'm a nervous wreck about Gabi going into labor. She's tiny, but then I remember she's about the size I was when I had y'all."

"You mentioned the doctor said Gabi had followed her guidance around nutrition. Jake found the best OB doctor in the city who specializes in multiples." I decide to change the subject so she doesn't continue to worry. "Need any help?"

"Actually, I could use some help with the pumpkin bars your dad likes so much. After debating, I catered the turkey, dressing, rolls, and two pies. Before I forget, Jake and Gabi will need to swing by around noon, so we're going to have an early dinner. You saw how slow she's moving... I don't want her to overdo it tomorrow."

The closer Gabi's due date approaches, the more my mom worries. Her experience with having twins herself adds to her anxiety. Over the years, she shared minor details. Recently, she mentioned she only dilated to six centimeters. She wanted to give birth naturally but realized the best option for Jake and me was to have a C-section. Dad and mom tried to have more children but after multiple miscarriages, they made peace with putting all of their love and energy into raising us.

Never once feeling shorted because I didn't have a sister. I loved being Jake's little sister. Jake never became annoyed when I followed him around like one of those wooden-toy dogs you pulled behind you holding the red string. Once we went to first grade, my mom insisted on separate rooms for us. Forced to make friends, I gradually began finding girls who loved playing soccer like me. Not the first time, I realize how insightful my mom was in raising us. I need to tell her... no better time than the present.

"Mom, I don't tell you enough, but I hit the mom jackpot when God was passing out moms. And now, you mother Gabi, which I love. You do everything so effortlessly. I don't know what I would do without you."

My mom looks at me and tears fill her eyes. "Jae, raising you and Jake has been the greatest joy of my life. I love being your mom. You didn't need to say anything, but I appreciate it." My mom gives me a big hug. "Now, tell me about your New York trip."

Travis and his eight-pack abs flash in my mind. We spent the day at the beach in Galveston before the summer crowd arrived last year. Gabi, Samantha, and I played volleyball against the guys. The game started friendly enough until we tied the guys in a winner takes the best of five games. Travis took off his shirt after he missed a spike I hit in his direction. My mind short-circuited in the moment. When did Travis get an eight-pack? What would he do if I ran my hands over his body? Acting nonchalant damn near killed me when all I wanted to do was climb him like a tree. Wait, what did my mom ask? New York... yes, New York.

"I plan to spend as much time as I can with Brittney. She mentioned in passing she plans to meet with the chef in the hotel Saturday morning so I decided to stay there. An added plus, the bridal store for our final fitting is down two city blocks. Time permitting, I may check in with a few of my NYU professors." Why am I rambling? Pausing before I continue takes a herculean effort, but I slow down and sound more like myself. "You know the holidays are my favorite time to be in New York. The Christmas decorations alone make the city feel magical."

"Sweetie, sounds like you're going to have a busy weekend. How are you flying?"

Prepared for my mom's question, I proactively booked a charter flight. My real reason, though, I didn't want word to get back to my parents that Travis flew with me. "This time around, I booked a private charter, not wanting to use the company jet in case anyone else needed it for work." I cringe as the lie rolls off my tongue. My mom knows everything about me, but I've withheld how much I've been struggling with this Jeremy debacle. Not wanting to add to her stress, she's already worried enough about the twins' arrival.

"Promise me you'll let me know you landed safely and tell Brittney to pass along to her mom that I will call her soon."

"I promise, mom."

Satisfied, my mom pulls the ingredients down from the pantry for the pumpkin bars and asks as an afterthought. "Do you need the recipe for the pumpkin bars?"

"No, I have it on my phone. Mind if I play the playlist that I made for you while we cook?"

"Now, that sounds divine. You have great taste in music. I'll let you in on a secret." I lean closer as she lowers her voice and says, "Your dad loves the playlists as much as I do. On our way to Bart and Lisa's, the jazz playlist started playing when his car connected to the phone. I just looked at him and gave him an '*I knew it*' look."

A laugh bubbles up and a huge smile spreads across my face. Dad loves teasing us just to be mildly disagreeable. He still makes mom laugh and her eyes light up any time he walks into the room. Not sure if love is in my future, but I know love exists... just one look at my parents' affectionate thirty-seven-year-old marriage proves soulmates exist.

When the phone rings, my twin sixth sense ratchets tenfold with worry after seeing Jake's name. "Hi Jake, is everything o...?"

Jake doesn't allow me to finish my question before he asks, "Is mom with you?"

"You are on speaker. Mom's right here. Is everything okay?"

"I'm on my way to Methodist Hospital now. Gabi has been having contractions all afternoon. The doctor thought we should come on in, especially since she's high risk with the twins."

My mom and I say at the same time. "We're on our way."

We find Jake pacing in the family waiting room. Jake's worry comes off in waves. I feel the intensity and wish there was something that I could do to help him. As a twin, we have always been able to know when we needed each other. Going off to college in New York when Jake stayed in Texas was the first time when we were truly apart. He would always know when I needed him. His calls would start with, "Jae, what's wrong?"

Not needing words, I open my arms. Jake walks into my embrace. He ducks his head since he towers over me by a good six inches. I hold Jake tight, his anxiety becoming mine. In a soothing motion, I rub my hand up and down his back, trying to ease some of his angst. He pulls away and looks at me with concerned eyes.

"Jae, I'm close to losing my shit right now, but this won't help Gabi. The nurse asked me to step out while they connect her to the monitor to measure her contractions."

"I know Jake. Gabi and the girls will be fine. You mentioned that her OB specializes in multiples. You have done everything to ensure Gabi and the girls have the best medical care and hospital possible. The Methodist women's center ranks in the top ten in the nation. Everything will be fine and you're not in this alone. We are here with you every step of the way."

I kiss Jake on the cheek and move over so mom can hug him. Momma G and Pops (Gabi's dad) stand next to mom. I walk over and give them both a hug. "Do you think the babies will come today?"

Momma G says, "They could. I know the doctor wants her to wait a few more weeks, but nature has a way of deciding for us."

"You're right. My nieces will arrive when they're ready." Before I can say anything else, Travis and CJ walk into the waiting room.

Travis eyes me intensely before he walks over to Jake. My mom joins me and Momma G. She hugs Momma G and says, "G, we both said the babies could come any day now."

Momma G nods and says with an apprehensive tone. "Chrissy, I'd hate to be right on this one. If the babies can wait a little longer, I'd be happy."

Jake leaves the room when the nurse comes to let him know he can follow her. We all huddle and have the same opinion: if the babies can wait a little while longer, they will be stronger. We quietly wait for an update from Jake. Not knowing what to do, I sit next to my mom and Momma G while the guys continue to stand.

I'm aware of every move Travis makes. When did this happen? This is new and I'm not sure I like it. Travis catches me looking and raises an eyebrow. Going for avoidance, I turn my chair with a haughty exhale and act like Travis doesn't exist.

After an hour, Jake comes back into the waiting room with a relieved look. "The contractions have stopped. Appears they were Braxton Hicks. Sorry everyone, but seems to be a false alarm. Momma G and Mom, Gabi would like to see y'all."

My dad squeezes my mom's hand as she silently follows Jake while holding onto Momma G's arm.

The anxiety weighing on the room like a three-hundred-pound gorilla lifts. Talking over each other with *what a relief* and *boy, I was worried there for a minute* statements.

With the excitement from yesterday, both moms spoke to Jake and Gabi to float the idea of bringing Thanksgiving to them. Gabi didn't want everyone to change their plans for her, but the moms insisted.

You'd think that we were at the Taste of Houston instead of a family Thanksgiving dinner. The dishes from both families spread across the counter buffet style, so everyone has their favorite dish. Mashed potatoes and brown-sugar-pecan-encrusted sweet potato casserole sit side-by-side. Traditional turkey and a creole-spiced fried turkey act as centerpieces for the twelve-seat dinner table. Whatever, everything looks delicious and works for me.

Gabi's grandparents joined us for the dinner, which is a rare treat. Every time I sit down with Madear, she showers me with smart quips and pearls of wisdom that help me as I'm navigating a new challenge. She treats me like another grandchild, loving me unconditionally. My heart bursts with love for her.

The families blended together well, despite Gabi and Jake's different backgrounds. The mom's shop together and grab lunch regularly; and the dads play golf and joined a cigar bar to relax after work at least once a month.

My gut wrenches as I wonder what the holidays will look like for me whenever I find my significant other. A yearning comes over me and an image of Travis flashes in my mind. Why... what the hell? This thing with Travis is nothing but a favor to help me get through my friend's wedding without going dateless. But why was he doing this? What was he getting out of this?

Jake walks up to me. "Sis, everything ok?"

"Yes," I stammer. "Yes, of course." I better change the subject before Jake uses his twin powers on me. "I love that we all came together for Thanksgiving instead of having you and Gabi travel to two different locations."

"Yeah, last night's close call really scared me, Jae. She means everything to me and the thought of her having to go through pain because of me..." Jake stops and shakes his head.

"I know Jake. You won't be going through this alone. Look around. We are all here for you and Gabi. On the plus side, you have backup if you need it from both moms."

"I can't wait to meet the girls. We went to our last Lamaze class this week. No surprise, we were the only couple having twins. If they come before New Year's Day, I'm ready and I know Gabi is ready. Gabi loves sitting in their nursery and still gushes about the mural you painted for the girls. Best gift ever, sis. You're so talented."

"Glad Gabi loves the design. I went into a zone once I started and love how the light pink and gray tones give the room a peaceful feeling. Are you ready, brother?"

My gaze tracks what has grabbed Jake's attention. Gabi struggles to get out of her chair. Jake jogs over to help her up and make sure she's steady before whispering in her ear. He nods and places his arm around her.

Gabi takes in the room. "Thank you, everyone, for coming. Your love and support mean the world to Jake and me. Not trying to be anti-social, but I need to lie down for a bit. Sleep evaded me all night—sleeping off and on for three hours. Please stay and keep Jake company. Don't feel the need to rush off."

We all tell her to take it easy and holler if she needs anything. Jake walks with Gabi tucked into his side as they head back to their bedroom. He doesn't have to tell us to make ourselves at home. Their home has quickly become the central gathering spot any time we get together. Doesn't matter if it's a holiday, sports events or just because, we find a reason to get together several times during the month.

The dessert table calls my name. I walk over in a trance. Yes, we have a dessert table with ten different desserts. The deep red strawberries look delicious. I contemplate having a piece of Madear's homemade pina colada cake. I should be worried about fitting into my maid of honor dress, but I swear the cake is speaking to me. While cutting a slice, I hear my dad say Travis's name. Not surprised, he stopped by. I keep my back turned, trying to delay facing him as long as possible. Sensing the air change, my reprieve ends. I fake a nonchalant look and say, "Hey, Travis."

Travis knows what I'm trying to do. With an amused smirk he says, "Hello, Jae," in a voice an octave deeper. Or was that my imagination?

Damn him, I feel myself go damp, but I've never backed away from a challenge. I look Travis directly in his eyes while taking a bite of my strawberry. When some juice lands on my bottom lip, I slowly drag my tongue to collect the juice and turn with a swing on my hips. When I hear him whisper, "Damn," I chuckle.

Travis

Damn, that move right there makes me imagine having my wicked way with her. My need for Jae is teetering on obsessive. Trying to rachet down my need, I shake my head. No way could I explain why I have a hard on, so I better get it together before I turn and walk back into the living room.

As I work to force down my need, I use the time to make the very important decision on what type of dessert should I have as the mouthwatering aromas waft around me. My sweet tooth wins in the end. I decide on three desserts (pecan pie, cake, and chocolate with cheesecake frosting brownies). Now my only other issue is how in the hell am going to get through this weekend without begging Jae to have a fake boyfriend with benefits arrangement?

Chapter Four

Travis

My eagerness to begin this weekend pulses through me. The sound of a car door slams in my driveway... finally. I grab my suitcase and lock my door after setting my alarm. Next to the shiny black Mercedes SUV, the driver waits. He pops open the trunk as I run my hand through my hair. Man, I feel nervous energy pump through me, similar to when I'm waiting for the organizer to announce the start of the triathlon. I place my bags in the trunk and sit in the back seat as I try to settle my nerves.

Jake and Gabi hosting Thanksgiving made my Thanksgiving with my parents more bearable. I used the excuse that I still had other stops to make and left after two painstaking hours.

My dad was more interested in what was on his phone while my mom tried to keep the conversation going with two men who didn't know how to talk to each other. Like I told mom, not sure why she thought it necessary to keep up the charade.

Jacqui tried to be more subdued than normal around me yesterday, but man oh man, when she ate that strawberry, I damn near swallowed my tongue. She may not realize it, but she's thrown down the gauntlet and I'm man enough to accept the challenge. We haven't talked about whether sex is on or off the table. After her display, I plan to broach the subject.

My bet... Jeremy didn't take the time to explore Jae's fiery sexual side that I know waits below the surface. I really want to be the man that makes all of her fantasies come to life. I've been using the memory of the kiss at the baby shower to fuel my sexual fantasies starring Jae. The workout my wrist received may have given me carpel tunnel, but I refuse to end this sexual hiatus unless it's with Jacqui.

Leaning my head back on the headrest, I close my eyes and immediately see an image of Jae laughing at something that Samantha said to her at Jake and Gabi's wedding. Her beauty never ceases to amaze me. She looked so carefree and her eyes sparkled like the Pacific blue Swarovski crystal earrings she wore. Jae's request to play her fake boyfriend gave me the opening that I'd been wracking my brain to figure out. With Jae back on the market, I calculated each approach only to end at the same roadblock... Jake. He knows me better than anyone, with one exception... I never shared with him my feelings for Jacqui. Now, I don't know what I feel for Jae, but I know I measure every single woman to her. Jae's the blueprint.

The car stops in front of a what appears to be the latest twelve-passenger Cessna private jet. While the driver hands my bags to the attendant, I walk inside of the cabin and whistle. With white oversized reclining seats, personal TVs, and window seat for every passenger, this jet puts my company's jet to shame.

After taking a sip from my pre-flight bourbon, I catch a whiff of Jacqui's signature jasmine and vanilla scent. My eyes lock on hers as I say in a voice a few octaves deeper (yes, the same voice that I used yesterday at Thanksgiving), "Hi Jae."

Apparently, Jacqui remembers all too well because I watch as the prettiest pinkish blush highlights her neck. Why did I have to notice her neck? I'd give anything to kiss her neck as I trail up behind her ear just to see what will happen. Would she shiver or would she moan as she dug her nails into my shoulder? This line of thinking will unveil an embarrassing situation any moment if I don't stop.

"Hey..." Jacqui has to clear her throat before she continues. "Hey Travis. Sorry for the early morning flight."

"You know this time doesn't bother me at all. Getting up early allows me to get a lot done." I meant the double meaning. I notice Jae glancing down at my lap before swiftly turning away. Saved by the flight attendant, who asked if she needed anything to drink.

Jae gets settled and what a beautiful view. Her curves remind me of an hour glass. She lost a ton of weight as she was preparing for her wedding. Never looking like a blushing bride, instead she looked manic and frazzled on most days. The idea of her thinking she needed to change her body for that asshole makes me clench my jaw. She was already perfect. No changes needed.

Neither one of us says anything as the crew goes through their safety spiel. I hand my empty glass to the flight attendant, then buckle up. As we taxi down the runway, Jae closes her eyes tight while white-knuckling the armrests. I gently pry her hand off and squeeze as I hold her hand. Wasn't until this moment that I remembered Jae hates taking off.

Once we level off, I reluctantly place her hand back on the armrest. I miss the contact already. I've never been a guy who enjoys holding hands until now. The women that I slept with knew I wasn't looking for a serious relationship. I made sure of that. Despite the obstacles, secretly, I fantasized Jae and I would marry, have at least two kids, and grow old together—a love for the record books.

I lean over so Jae can hear me and say in a low voice, "Jae, are you okay now?"

Deep blue eyes snag my attention. "Yes, Travis. Thanks, by the way. I've tried everything to get over this fear." She blushes when she says, "I even tried hypnosis. Attended a fear of flying course. Tried visualization." She shrugs. "It's all bullshit."

"No worries. I'm just glad I was here. What do you do when you're not flying with family?"

"A travel blanket, my secret hack. I lay it over my lap and hands." Her smile brightens as she adds, "I'm very proud of myself for coming up with this simple hack. Works like a charm."

"So, what's the plan when we get to New York?"

"Apologies upfront. We have a pretty busy morning. We need to head directly to the gallery to approve the artwork placement. She sent me pictures and videos, but I'd feel less anxious about tonight if I can see how my painting flows with the exhibit."

Determined to show Jae, I won't let her down. I silently vow to show Jae what Jake and CJ already know... she can depend on me. I finally have the opportunity for Jae to see the real me... a man who she can count on—no matter what. Not the womanizing caricature Jae has associated with me for far too long. Over the years, I acted like I didn't care that she saw me this way, and maybe that was true when I thought I would never get my shot. Well, I care... I care a helluva lot.

My answer comes easy. "Done. What's next after that?"

"An appointment with another curator comes next. I interned at his gallery my junior year of NYU, so I reached out, letting him know I'd be in town. He's squeezing me in for a thirty-minute meeting to catch up and hopefully discuss featuring my pieces in the future."

"Jae—wow, I didn't realize you were serious about painting."

Jacqui

I take a deep breath before answering. "Nobody does. With Jake and Gabi about to have the twins, my mom has been a nervous wreck, so I haven't wanted to bother her with my dream to become a full-time artist." Before continuing, I pause, then say, "I guess I have Jeremy to thank. I've always wanted to take my art to another level, but stopped dedicating the time needed until recent events. Early after the broken engagement, I painted here and there. Now, I paint practically every evening after work."

"I remember seeing some of your sketches when we were in college. You're a talented artist. I'm happy for you."

"Yeah, well, I may need backup when I finally find the courage to tell my parents. I want to take a lesser role in the company–one that's not so high profile and maybe even a reduced schedule. My dad's been dropping hints he wants me to shadow Rob, our chief operating officer, since Rob announced his retirement for next year."

He smirks with a teasing glint in his eyes. "I see it written all over your face... not your jam, huh?"

My stomach knots just thinking of a future filled with boring staff and strategy meetings. Unable to keep the disdain from my voice, I speak from the heart. "Not in the least. I hoped my dad would have taken the hint when I selected the most creative role in the company, besides architecture."

With more sincerity than I'm surprised to see, Travis confirms by saying, "Whenever, wherever you need me, I'll be there."

Travis amazes me with his attentiveness. When he says he'll be there for me, my gut tells me I can believe him. I wonder what other surprise he has up his sleeve. Before any wicked thoughts can form, I slam the door.

Hard. Later... yes, much later behind closed doors when I have time to explore.

"Appreciate it, Travis. What do you plan to do with your free time while we're in New York?"

"One of my friends from law school ended up settling in Manhattan. We plan to grab a beer tomorrow, but don't worry... I'll be looking for your text if things change and you need me."

When Travis says things like this, I wonder what's changed. I've never known Travis to be anything but self-centered. No, my impression formed from observations over the years, but I may not have the full picture... he's always been there for my brother, Jake, and CJ. Those three are more like brothers than friends. Would he really be there for me if I needed him at a moment's notice?

I feel Travis's intense stare and look up to see the heat in his eyes, but there's something more there. I can't decipher what it could be. What I wouldn't do to read Travis's mind. I see warmth, but how? We may be in each other's orbit, but barely. Our timing has never really synced. I am usually leaving my parents' house as Travis stops by to visit. We overlap, but never for long.

Over the years, I've noticed how close Travis and my dad have become. Travis seeks my dad's guidance on decisions before he makes a move. Unsolicited, my mom informed me Travis invested in a local up-and-coming brewery that specialized in IPAs. Apparently, Travis was multifaceted. I wonder where else he's multifaceted and feel a throb where a throb has no business throbbing. Bad, bad thoughts as I feel my nipples harden and my face flush. Thank God we're not sitting across from each other. Pretty sure Travis would have noticed.

Not as lucky as I thought, Travis leans over and whispers in my ear, "Penny for your thoughts."

When I turn, our lips are so close I just need to lean a little more to give Travis the scorching kiss from my dream last night. We were back in the wine cellar. Our kiss went from a sizzle to incendiary. Travis had his hand on my hip and pulled me flush against his muscular chest and well-defined abs. I could feel every inch of him. He made his presence known. When he backed me against the wall, I wrapped my legs around his waist. While kissing down my neck, he drifted his hand up my thigh and then... my alarm went off.

I never wanted to chuck my phone across the room so badly. Unfortunately, I had another problem. I didn't have enough time to take care of all the wound-up sexual need. Lord, how am I going to get through this weekend without having my wicked way with him? We have a two-bedroom suite, but with only a living room between, the barrier may not be enough. What would Travis do if I told him I wanted a fake boyfriend with benefits arrangement? Only until the wedding, though, then we go back to our normal lives where we barely know the other exists.

I step back and take a shuttered breath before starting. "Nothing. I remembered there's something that I need to do this weekend, that's all."

"Well, don't forget that I'm here for you, Jae. For anything... anything you need."

I close my legs tight to stop the pulsating. Apparently, my lady parts love this idea... jumping up and down, clapping and saying, '*Pick him! Pick him! He looks like he'd be a ton of fun.*'

My prim and proper side wins this round as I hear myself say, "Yeah, well, I can't think of anything at the moment."

His dark chuckle promises something sizzling. Hot. Wild. I can even hear his taunting *liar, liar, pants on fire* chant.

Chapter Five

Jacqui

True to his word, Travis handled each stop like a pro. I didn't catch him fidgeting, looking at his watch impatiently or huffing loudly. We're checked into The Plaza's two-bedroom suite and I'm nervous, like a nervous thirteen-year-old waiting on her first kiss during a game of *Seven Minutes in Heaven*. "Well..." I clear my throat, "if you don't mind, I'll take the room with the bear claw tub. I've been dreaming about that tub since I booked this suite."

"Is that all you've been dreaming about, Jae?"

Why does he do that? Why does he make his voice sound all deep and sultry? How much can a girl take? I spin and walk, head held high, to my room as I hear Travis challenge me to reveal my secrets. I need to come up with a game plan while I shower and try to relax before tonight's art show.

The door closes on a light snick of the lock when I'd rather slam the door shut. Instead, I close the door and lean my back against the door while my hand is still holding the doorknob with a tight death grip. I repeat over and over... just take some deep breaths. Remember, you practice yoga three times a week, for God's sake. As I close my eyes, trying to find my center, Travis and his smile with promises of a sinful good time flash in my mind. Frustrated, I walk angrily to the bathroom as I take off my clothes. The bathrobe hanging on a lingerie hanger from the hook next to the stand-alone shower takes the brunt of my frustration. Yanking the robe off the hanger while shoving my arms into the sleeves gives me a moment to calm down.

After tying the robe, a little too tight, I bend over to fill the bathtub, fighting fantasies of Travis bending me over and having his way with me. I need to get laid, that's all there is to it. Sad to realize it's been over six months since I had mediocre sex. Unacceptable. I need someone who will fuck me so good I forget my name. I deserve to have not only good sex but the best sex of my life.

My instincts tell me Travis could be just the man to give me what I've never had. He has big D energy oozing off him like the heat on the horizon of a blistering hot day. Yeah, Travis wouldn't disappointment. Now, to convince him we can have a fake relationship with benefits arrangement.

The tub fills with copious bubbles as I remove my robe and step into the tub. I needed this before tonight's event. Still pinching myself, my friend thinks my piece will sell fast. This won't be my first piece, but this could be the first piece where the sale would be around five figures.

On a whim, I resurrected my old pen name from college, Liza J. A combination of my grandmother's name, Elizabeth and my first initial. Refusing to use my family name, I want any success to come from my hard work. My friends know my background, but they help me keep my worlds separate.

My eyes drift close as I realize I'm falling asleep. With great difficulty, I remove myself from the bubble bath. A nap in the tub would leave me all wrinkly. Yawning again, I barely make it to the bed before face planting.

My alarm blares at five. Boy, I must have been exhausted. Those two hours flew by. After washing my face and brushing my teeth, I head to the living room to find Travis watching a football game. "Hey. Just wanted to make sure that you remembered we will need to leave at six thirty to arrive on time."

"I don't need much time to get ready. There normally are only hors d'oeuvres at these things. Do you need me to order room service so you can at least eat something before we head out?" he asks, clicking off the television and giving me his full attention.

Huh, that's really sweet. Another indication, my assumptions may have been way off about Travis. "Thanks, Travis. You know you're right. I'll probably be too nervous to eat once I'm at the event. Can you order me a salad with grilled salmon? They have the best lemon vinaigrette dressing."

Travis

"Sure, I'll place the order now and ask for a five thirty delivery time. Will this give you enough time to get ready?"

"Yeah, I'll get everything done but my makeup and dress before the meal arrives. Oh, and Travis... thanks so much for coming this weekend. This means a lot... I mean, what you're doing means a lot to me."

"Anytime Jae."

Glad to see her earlier shyness wearing off. I wonder if she even realized that she stood there wearing nothing but her bathrobe. Her robe didn't gap, but my imagination conjured up visions of me testing the weight of one breast while sucking on the nipple of her other breast in my mouth. Not the first time since our trip began where I noticed Jacqui's amazing body. What's wrong with me? For years, Jacqui has been nothing more than Jake's little sister, knowing that she would never be mine. Ever since her broken engagement, it's like something inside me broke open... I want to take my shot.

Jake will kick my ass if I break her heart... hell, he'll kick my ass for touching his sister. He should be more worried about my heart getting broken. I've never been in these waters... never been in a relationship... never been in love. Would I even know what love looked like if it was staring me in my face?

After ordering our dinner, I head to my room to lay my suit on the bed and grab my shoes from the suitcase. My phone sits charging on the nightstand. As I picked it up to check for messages, I noticed two missed calls and decide to call my colleague. "Max, saw your calls. Any issues with the deal?"

"Hey Travis, I found a potential issue with one patent. Do you have time over the weekend to review and give me your opinion?"

"Tomorrow late morning works. Let me take a look and call you around noon. Will this work for your schedule?"

"The timing works perfectly. Sarah is taking the kids to an indoor trampoline park for a birthday party. I'll be ready. Thanks, man. Sorry to interrupt your holiday weekend, but there was something about those patents that kept bothering me. I couldn't let it go."

"Appreciate it, Max." A knock sounds at the door. "Gotta go. I'll review and talk to you tomorrow."

Jacqui and I walk into the living room at the same time. "I've got it and will handle the tip." After opening the door, I ask for the dinner to be setup on the dining table.

Jacqui looks at the setup and smiles when she notices I ordered her favorite white wine. Well, I guessed it was her favorite, since she had a bottle when I went to her house.

"Travis, how did you know this was my favorite white wine?"

I lift a shoulder like it's no big deal. "You had a glass when I came over last weekend."

She leans over and kisses me on the cheek. "Thanks, Travis. It's actually very sweet and thoughtful. A glass will help calm me down a bit."

I pull out her chair and need to clear my throat. The chaste kiss caused a yearning so deep. The desire to take the kiss to another level tugs on me like the gravitational pull. All I can say is, "Have a seat." We eat in silence for a few minutes, giving me time to get myself together. Once I feel more in control, I ask about her last time in New York. "I haven't been to New York during the holiday season in a good five plus years. How about you?"

"My girlfriends from college and I get together once a year for a girl's trip. About two years ago, we met in New York for a three-day weekend—crammed in three Broadway shows, a spa day and more shopping than necessary. One positive, I got all my Christmas shopping done that trip... bonus. Everyone loved their gift."

After taking a sip of wine, I contemplate my next question. My interest stems from curiosity. Jae and I know the basics about each other but nothing substantial. "Sounds like fun. Did you take all the prerequisite New York holiday pictures?"

Jae shakes her head while setting down her wine. "No, having lived here for practically five years, those pictures always felt like such a touristy thing to do."

I chuckle, shake my head and open my mouth to talk when Jacqui interjects with an amused glint in her eyes like she's trying to hold back laughing. Then with a conspiratorial whisper, she leans closer to me. The jasmine scent lingers as she leans back in her chair. "Travis, do you have a secret? Did you and your bros take some of those pictures?" She leans back to scrutinize me further, then nods after she concludes. "I bet you did. I bet you have those pictures on your phone right now. Am I right?"

My face heats but I refuse to concede. Bet placed; I hedge. "I can neither confirm nor deny."

Jacqui and I hold each other's gaze for a beat, then two when I notice her breathing change. I know that look... Jacqui wants me. I clear my throat and search for a safer topic. "Have you talked to your mom since you arrived?"

"Yeah, but it was brief. After letting her know that I arrived safely, she confirmed Gabi continues to rest like the doctor ordered."

Jacqui looks at her watch. "Oh, I forgot to tell you. At tonight's event, can you call me by my nickname? My artist's name is Liza J, but Jae should suffice."

"Nice. You took part of your grandmother's first name. Ingenious... and it suits you, by the way."

"Thanks Travis. I better go finish getting ready before we're late. We don't have too far to go, but traffic on a Friday evening in Manhattan frustrates even a true New Yorker. Can you be ready in thirty?"

"Of course, anything for you, Jae," I say with a smile on my face.

Jacqui

The butterflies have returned, mostly from excitement. Many of the female artists featured tonight could have their own show. To be considered in the same category as them, I just have to pinch myself.

After applying my makeup and curling my hair, I walk back into my bedroom to dress. The fitted, barely see-through black with glimmering crystal dress fits me like a glove. With deep scalloped cuts down the front, the V stops right above my navel. Showing this amount of cleavage, the dress is more daring than what I'd normally wear. When I found the dress, my heart leapt excitedly as I pictured myself wearing the dress at this event. The dress makes me feel sexy, powerful, and ready to take on the world. The best part, seeing Travis's reaction. I could have warned him, but what would be the fun in that?

One problem... I need help with my dress. After slipping into the clear, strappy five-inch heels and grabbing my clutch, I walk back into the living room. Turned slightly away, Travis clips his cuff links.

"Travis, can you...?" My voice sounds soft and hesitant to my ears. Get it together Jae.

Before I finish, Travis turns, whistles, and damn near growls. "Damn Jae. You look amazing. Are you trying to get me arrested tonight?"

Wasn't sure of the effect the dress would have on Travis, but I needed his compliment. Not only feeling sexy, I feel pretty and flirty too. My confidence skyrockets. "Now, now, Travis, you expect me to believe that you can't handle this little ole dress?"

He stalks toward me with his five o'clock shadow while blatant male satisfaction beams across his face. In a voice dripping with promises of a fantasy-filled night, Travis brushes his hand over my hip. "Oh, I can handle this dress. I don't think I can handle *you* in this dress."

Playfully patting Travis's lapel while saying, "I have faith in you, but before we leave, I need a favor. Can you finish zipping me up?"

Travis walks around me and stops abruptly when he gets to my back. His warm breath sends a delicious shiver down my back when he says in a mesmerized voice, "You don't have on a bra. I hope I'm not being a neanderthal, but how are you keeping everything from ummm..."

I look over my shoulder as I see Travis concentrating intently on how in the hell am I not having a wardrobe malfunction. "You're cute when you're flustered, Travis. Think of this as a modern-day magic trick. Trust me, I have everything under control."

Almost like he's in a trance, he takes his index finger and drags it up my spine as he slowly zips my dress. I quiver from the touch. What's that saying about playing with fire? If I have any chance of surviving this fake relationship, my self-preservation requires me to remember who I'm flirting with. Travis is a full grown, red-blooded alpha male. And my brother's best friend.

He steps back and shakes his head like he's trying to clear his thoughts. "My lady, your carriage awaits."

Travis

I thank God for small favors. Draping my coat over my arm conceals my hard on. Jacqui's beauty always captivated me, but this dress... Smoke show doesn't even come close to describing how damn good she looks. My knees buckled when I noticed the subtle see through aspect of the dress. No two ways about it. I plan to be by her side all night.

The drive to the New Museum of Contemporary Art took us close to an hour. The red carpet cushions our short walk into the museum. Jacqui's friend, Emma, greets us. "Liza J, you're right on time. I'll take your coats. My assistant will handle the coat check while you mingle. Have fun."

I wrap my arm around Jacqui's waist as she leads me through the crowd. When a guy I don't know leans in to kiss her cheek, I pull Jacqui slightly back but she stops me and whispers, "Behave."

Not deterred, the man grabs Jae's hand and brings it to his lips for a kiss. "Mark, how have you been? I heard your one-man exhibition went well."

Mark looks more like a hipster rock star, instead of an artist, wearing more hair products than any woman in the room and tight black leather pants. "Very well, actually. They booked me for another exhibition next year. How long are you in town?"

I may have growled, not sure, but ask me if I care. If Jacqui will have me, I want the opportunity to see if we can make this fake relationship real. I just need time to show Jacqui I am not the man whore she thinks I am.

Once Mark left, I lean over. "Do you want something to drink?"

Jae looks wide eyed like she doesn't feel she belongs here. "Actually, a chardonnay sounds divine right now."

Acting on instinct, I pull her close to my side and whisper in her ear. "You belong here. Your painting rivals the others. You've got this. Besides, you're not alone... you have me. I'll be right back."

Jae gives me an appreciative smile and surprises me with a kiss on the check. "Thanks Travis. You knew exactly what I needed in this moment."

Jacqui

Tonight has been a dream come true. After only being here for an hour, several attendees gathered around my painting. Emma engaged the group to hear their interpretation of the piece. Awed by the feelings my piece evoked, I shared they were all correct. My emotions were all over the place when I painted this piece... pouring my hurt, anger, disappointment and resilience into every stroke. The patron who purchased the painting even stopped me as we were leaving to say I moved her to tears.

Painting, as long as I can remember, has been my safe place, a cocoon of love and happiness. The common icebreaker question, *'in a fire, if you could only take one item, what would it be?'*, hands down my paint brushes. Over the years, as I traveled to different destinations, I found local artisans who use old world methods to make handmade paint brushes. Having the right brush in my hands feels like an extension of my soul.

Looking over to Travis sitting quietly, deep in thought, I'm struck with the realization that I really enjoyed having him with me tonight. More attentive than I would have thought he could be, holding my hand, wrapping me close to his side, or standing to the side while I spoke. His five o'clock shadow changed as the night progressed into something more delicious. What I wouldn't do to run my hands over his chiseled jawline?

I whisper, "Travis." When he turns, his look smolders. The back seat of the Mercedes feels more intimate, like we're all alone. I lean into Travis and kiss him softly. As I pull back, Travis wraps his arm around my back and threads his fingers into the nape of my neck. I automatically open for the kiss. When Travis takes over the kiss, his tongue touches mine. Drowning under the sensual haze Travis creates, he kisses me senseless until we both have to come up for air.

The truth stares me in the face... I want this man, like *now*. We can't get back to the hotel fast enough. Hallelujah, the driver announced that we have arrived.

Travis places his hand on my lower back as we walk through the lobby. We both walk with a purpose to the elevator. Once inside, I use this opportunity to let Travis know how much his presence meant to me tonight. "Travis, thank you again for coming tonight. Having you there for support went a long way in reducing my nerves. I could just be in the moment. Still can't believe that my painting sold. Best-case scenario, I thought the painting would be on display through the winter before being boxed and shipped back to me."

"You're a talented artist, Jacqui." When I look at him skeptically, he continues, "No, you really are good. Able to witness you in your element, doing something you were born to do, filled me with pride. Consider me a fan."

I step into Travis and ask, "Is that all you are, Travis… a fan?"

Travis grabs my waist as he bends and kisses me deeply. This kiss is different, like I matter. I stroke his tongue when the elevator dings.

Travis

Without hesitating, I hold Jae's hand and walk with a determined stride to our suite. After closing the door, I kiss her again with urgency while removing our coats as we walk into her room. As we cross the threshold to her room, I step back while breathing like I've run a two-mile sprint when a moment of clarity hits me. "Jae, wait, you've had a few drinks. I… I can't… we can't, not like this."

Jacqui looks down dejected, maybe even a little embarrassed. Taking two fingers to lift her chin, I see rejection in her eyes. "Hey, look at me. This is not a rejection, Jae. I want you so bad right now." I take her hand and place it over my crotch. "Do you feel how hard I am? You're gorgeous. I just don't want you to wake up in the morning and regret anything."

Light returns to her eyes. Her next statement damn near brings me to my knees. "Travis, I want you. I want you *now*. Don't worry about me regretting anything. I won't have any regrets."

My determination stutters for a moment but I fortify my resolve. "I respect you more than you know. This will probably kill me, but I'm going to head to my bed."

Jae takes her index and middle fingers as she traces my steel outline. "Are you sure, Travis? I know how hard this must be for you?"

For a brief moment, I close my eyes and enjoy her exploration. I groan as I step back, turn, and walk to my bedroom. "Night, Jae."

After tossing and turning all night, I put on my winter running gear and head out for a five-mile run in Central Park. Running outside in New York fills my lungs with refreshing cold air. Living in Texas, the number of opportunities to experience the perfect running weather happens less than a few weeks a year.

No surprise, early morning joggers flood the path. My thoughts keep returning to how Jacqui felt in my arms last night. Our chemistry combusts at off-the-chart levels. The energy between us pulses. Every time I kiss her, my need goes from zero to a hundred similar to a teenager surprised the prettiest girl in the school likes him. My feet felt encased in concrete blocks as I trudge back to my room after leaving a willing Jacqui to sleep alone. Buzzed sex curbs a need, but I want Jacqui sober when I make love to her.

I stumble, make love? Really?? I'm not even sure if Jacqui wants anything but sex and a fake boyfriend out of this arrangement. Why would she? She sat front-row seat to the parade of women... names long forgotten.

Do I even know how to love? My own parents, who's DNA I share, gave sparse slithers of their time over the years. My dad only started talking to me in high school on a regular basis because he was interested in my plans for college. He hoped I would follow in his footsteps as a real estate developer.

Each year living in their house got me closer to the day when I could finally leave for college and never look back. Unfortunately, the belief, love comes with strings attached, lingers. My own parents made no secret their marriage brokered like a business deal. My dad needed access to the affluent business owners my mom's father kept out of reach until after they married.

The run takes a frantic pace as I try to run away from these thoughts. Going down this path always puts me in a sour mood. When I walk back into the suite I don't want to be in this frame of mind. Jacqui mentioned she needs to meet with the bridal party but the time escapes me. If she's still in the suite, my disposition needs to be upbeat.

Surprised to see the hotel coming into view, my pace slows as I begin my cool down.

My phone digs with a notification as I walk into our suite. Not seeing Jacqui at first, I pause to appreciate Jae in the sexy, fitted off-white above-the-knee sweater dress with knee-high boots. Damn, she looks good. "Hey, gorgeous. Love your outfit. I like New York Jacqui. You dress differently here."

She looks down and acts like a piece of lint sticks to her tights. The shy blush on her cheeks makes me record for future reference to compliment her often. My frown fierce wondering what damage Jeremy did.

A slight smile spreads as Jae tilts her head. "Thanks, but I had to up my game. Several of my friends could easily be models if they wanted the jet-set lifestyle. You'll get to meet my friends at the wedding."

With Jae sharing this small insight, an invisible thread stitches us closer to each other. "Well, you fit right in."

"Do you have big plans today?"

After grabbing an ice-cold water from the mini bar, I lean my hip on the credenza against the wall. "Actually, I have some legal briefs to review and an issue with one of my pending acquisitions that needs to be addressed. Should take to lunch time then I plan to meet my friend for lunch and grab a quick drink in the bar. Hope you're not too tired with today's events. I made eight o'clock dinner reservations for us. Will this give you enough time to get back and relax a bit before we head out?"

Jae widens her eyes in surprise. "Travis, eight o'clock works. I'll be back in plenty of time. I better run. Brittney, a.k.a. 'the bride,' asked if I could meet her in a ballroom downstairs to review selections for the reception before we head to our final fittings."

With a casual stride, I walk towards Jacqui. She eyes me with suspicion, probably thinking I plan to wipe my sweat on her. Now what kind of gentleman would I be if I did? After placing a chaste kiss, I head to my room as I say, I "Have fun!"

After a shower, I ordered an egg white spinach omelet with mushrooms and coffee, then began reading through the patents. Few issues captured, I switched to the legal briefs since I still had an hour before I had to call Mark.

Mark and I connected on the potential issues. Between the two of us, I felt we had a comprehensive list of the areas that need to be addressed. As the lead attorney, I owned analyzing all aspects of the acquisition, including any red flags that need to be researched and assessed. Next week, we meet with senior leadership to provide an update and confirm if we recommend continuing with the next phase of due diligence or walk away from the deal.

As the head strategist and architect of the deal, this acquisition has the potential to catapult my company as the leader in renewable energy. Earlier in my career, I wanted to hear my dad say how proud he was... now, I no longer look for his affirmation. Jake's dad tells me often how proud he is of the man I've become.

After lunch with Josh, I came back to the room and turned on the TV to see Die Hard had just started. Over the years, I've argued with folks who don't consider Die Hard a Christmas movie. My argument usually wins by pointing out the obvious... the terrorists take hostages attending a company Christmas party, just happens to have some cool stunts and shit that blows up. The door clicks open. Jae walks into the room as I look over my shoulder.

She takes one look at the TV and says, "I love Die Hard, the best Christmas movie ever! Be right back. I'm going to get into something more comfortable."

The wry smirk I try to hide belies my shock in her announcement. "My sentiments exactly."

Who knew Jae was a Die-Hard fan? We appear to have more in common than I realized. Makes me wonder what else we have in common. Another confirmation, I don't know much about Jacqui. With tonight's dinner, I plan to remedy this issue.

Jacqui walks back in wearing snowflake covered pajama pants and a cute long sleeve light blue shirt that stops right above her belly button showing a dainty heart-shaped diamond belly ring. My mouth waters. Jae is full of surprises. I wonder what else she's been keeping under wraps. Later... tonight can't come fast enough. "Nice pajama bottoms. How did everything go?"

"Great. I calmed Brittney down. She was worried about the appetizers after discovering several family members on her father's side are allergic to shrimp. We spoke to the head chef. He understood the concern and promised to change out the problematic hors d'oeuvres."

Jae turns slightly in the couch to face me and continues, "Fitting went well, but Brittney let me in on a secret. She's a little over four weeks pregnant and didn't want anyone else to know. I discreetly spoke to the bridal shop manager when we arrived. Last thing we wanted was the seamstress to innocently announce her dress needed to be taken out."

Impressed how Jae takes care of the people in her life. The admiration conveys in my voice. "You're a good friend. She's lucky to have you."

Jae shakes her head dismissing my statement. Just another thing to like about Jacqui… her humility. "I'm the lucky one. Brittney is my sister from another mister."

Before I can say something else, Jacqui interrupts me, "Look, I love this part."

We both watched, enthralled, as Bruce worked through each challenge one by one. This isn't the first time I've recognized how easy it is to just be with Jae. The silence isn't awkward… we don't feel the need to fill the silence with mindless conversation. When Jacqui leans her head on my shoulder, I enjoy having her in my arms. Usually alone when I'm at home, I'm finding that I really like Jacqui all up in my space. This feels natural, like she's supposed to be here.

When Die Hard Two started, I looked down to see Jacqui had fallen asleep. Since we had over two hours until our dinner reservations, I stand, slip Jae into my arms, and walk to her bed. As I lay Jae down, she mumbles, "Watch out McClane" and snores lightly.

Probably already way over my head, I smile as I close the door to her bedroom, finding even her snore cute.

Chapter Six

Jacqui

At first, I lay here disoriented. Darkness shows through the curtails and I'm in my bed. I must have fallen asleep on Travis. What time is it? Oh crap, six o'clock! Suddenly wide awake, I jump out of bed, splash some water on my face and brush my teeth before going to find Travis.

He's where I left him, watching another Die-Hard movie. "Are they having a marathon or something?"

Travis looks over his shoulder and lands on my belly ring with a heated glance that flashes briefly. He clears his throat then casually says, "Yeah, apparently. How was your nap?"

Before I answer, a plan begins to form. Usually, fine with allowing a guy make the first move, I decide to be bold... maybe even try a sprinkle of seduction. "Good thanks. What time do we need to be ready to leave for our dinner reservations?"

"It's not too far from the hotel, but I've asked the driver to arrive at seven to pick us up."

One last thing I need to know before I finalize my transformation into sexy, siren Jae. "Do you know the dress code?"

Travis thinks for a moment then ticks off the guidelines by touching his first three fingers with the index finger from his other hand. "No jeans or tennis shoes; oh, and guys need to wear a jacket."

My nipples bead in anticipation of spending the evening with Travis. "Nice. I love getting dressed up for dinner. I'll be ready by seven."

"Sounds good, Jae. I'll start getting dressed as well."

After taking a quick shower, I decide on smoky eyes with a natural look and my black sheer La Perla matching set to wear underneath. Since my dress is a fitted off-the-shoulder black Versace logo dress, I didn't want any lines from my underwear, so the thong won. What will Travis think? Now that I know his no drinking rule, you better believe I'm only having water tonight with dinner. My dry spell ends tonight. A shiver deliciously races through my body... primed waiting for all of Travis's attention focused on me.

Travis has neatly trimmed his five o'clock shadow from yesterday. My clit throbs at the sight. I need to get it together before he can tell that I'm already aroused.

As I approach, his scorching gaze takes in my dress. When I was with Jeremy, my weight dropped over thirty pounds that I was rail thin. My curves are back, and the wolfish expression on Travis's face shows he likes what he sees.

"Jae, you look... you look amazing. I could kiss you right now."

My sass takes center stage. "What's stopping you?"

Travis whispers, "Nothing," as he lowers his head. I open for him, not even trying to play coy. When Travis wraps his arms around me, I'm flush to his front. He grabs my tongue and sucks gently. He turns his head while threading his fingers at the nape of my neck. My need makes me bolder than I have ever been. Kissing Travis, a new experience I want to take the time to explore. No one... no one has ever kissed me with so much passion.

Travis kisses me a little longer before pulling back and placing his forehead on mine. We both take big gulps of air. Closing my eyes to settle myself. We could just stay in. Before I can recommend, Travis says, "Let's go before I cancel our dinner reservations."

My hand rubs along his hardened length and I ask the obvious question. "Are you sure? We can stay in."

Travis groans, removes my hand painstakingly slow, and looks at me earnestly. "I really want to take you on a date."

When I blink my wide eyes in disbelief, he continues, "Jae, you and I barely speak whenever we're in the same vicinity. Jake only gives me headline worthy updates. Let's go to dinner. It should embarrass me to say, but I've been looking forward to this since I agreed to join you this weekend. I want to get to know you better."

For a moment, I'm speechless. That was the last thing I expected him to say. "You're right. Going out on the town will be nice, especially seeing all the holiday decorations again." With regret, I grab my coat and clutch as we head to the elevator.

Travis

We walk to the elevator as I place my hand on Jacqui's lower back. She feels like mine. I'm not sure how to maneuver in these waters, but fake boyfriend or not, I like how I feel when I'm with her. She makes me feel like I can take on the world. My friends and mom can always depend on me, but I've never extended this to another woman. I want to be that man for Jacqui.

My friends even affectionately call me Tin Man. Somewhere along the way, I identified with the Tin Man, believing my heart only beats to keep me alive and nothing else. Turning this fake relationship into something more makes me want to have the courage to fight for Jacqui. I drop my head for a moment and take a deep breath, trying to return to the present.

Jacqui places her hand on my arm. "Is everything okay?"

"Yeah, yeah, everything's good."

Saved by the bell, we finally arrive at the lobby just as Jacqui's stomach growls. I chuckle, "Let's get you fed."

The maître d leads us to our table with a window view of Times Square. The sway of Jacqui's hips kept me mesmerized until I noticed a guy turn his head as Jae walked by. I gave him a look that said, *'too bad, so sad, but she's going home with me.'*

Jae's smile brightens as she turns to look across the skyscape. "Travis, love this view. I haven't been to this restaurant in years. If you've never eaten here before, you're in for a treat."

Ignoring the outside view, I appreciate every aspect of Jae... her cute nose, sparkling eyes, and light freckles on her cheeks. "You're right. The view takes my breath away." The smile as she tilts her head to the side confirms she realized I wasn't talking about Times Square. We both order water and decide on an appetizer to start. "I feel like I know very little about you, even though we've known each other since ninth grade. While at NYU, did you live on campus?"

She looks surprised by my question, but settles back comfortably into her chair before answering. "Mom and dad wouldn't have it any other way. Brittney and I were roommates from freshman year to when we graduated. She's from Scarsdale, not too far from Manhattan, so we would hang at her home on the weekends when we didn't have a paper or project due."

My mind flashes to an eighteen-year-old Jae with long wavy hair pulled back in her signature high ponytail. "Why NYU?" I joke. "Was it to get as far away from Jake as possible?"

Her throaty laugh makes my dick twitch. "I came to visit the campus and fell in love with the school. Trying to figure out my major was tricky. I finally ended up with a double major in digital communications and fine arts. With every art class that I took, I felt pulled between getting a degree to work at my grandfather's firm and exploring art to express myself."

Jae's talent impresses me. "Your art is amazing, especially the mural you painted in the twin's nursery. It gives the room a tranquil feel. Besides painting, do you have other forms of art that you do?"

Jae leans towards me as she begins to share her passion. "I dabble with pottery, but painting is my passion. The summer of my junior year, I took a painting immersion course in Paris... the best summer of my life. We even had after-hours access to the Louvre."

Man, I'm in trouble. Her inner light shines as she talks about her passion... all I want is to find a way to keep her talking so I can bask in all the things I find absolutely intriguing about Jae. "I remember hearing that you were in Paris for a summer course. Seeing how you light up any time you talk about your art, I'm glad that you did something that I can tell you absolutely love."

She blushes and slants her head as she absorbs the praise. Jae's family celebrates her accomplishments, but I'm wondering if she was able to share this side of herself with Jeremy. His self-absorbed nature probably left little room for him to recognize the remarkable woman right in front of him. "Thanks, Travis. How about you? How do you like being a lawyer?"

If Jae had asked me this question as I prepared to graduate with my bachelor's degree, I would have answered law school will give me three more years to decide my career path. The extra time allowed me to explore different law fields until I discovered intellectual property. "One day I may open my practice, but now working as a corporate attorney fits me. As a senior attorney, I work on multiple strategic deals at once, which works for me. I get bored easily, but with each deal being different, my work continues to challenge me."

Jae listens intently before answering. "This answers a lot of questions that I've had over the years... you always seem like you're busy. Well, besides your day job, I know you are a triathlete and play city soccer. Tell me something that few people know about you."

Before answering, I hesitate and debate whether I should share my private secret. Only Jake, his dad, and CJ know. "I work with wood in my spare time. I even have a wood shop in my backyard."

Jae smiles and scoots closer to the table like she wants the juicy details. "Wow! I would have never guessed. What do you build? Have you sold any of your pieces?"

Her excitement causes me to puff my chest with pride. "I build furniture, mostly dining and coffee tables. A dealer takes my pieces on consignment. Earlier this week, I heard from the dealer that one client would like to order a custom headboard with matching nightstands."

"That's great news! I'd love to see your work."

My smile spreads as I realize I really want to share this side of myself with Jae. "Now *that* I can do." As our food arrives, we continue with our conversation. Not the first time I notice how easily I can talk to Jae. Getting to know Jacqui has been the highlight of my weekend.

Jacqui

The elevator dings announcing its arrival. Once the elevator closes, I lean into Travis and kiss his jaw. "I don't want the evening to end. I could be coy, but I don't want to play games. Any issues with adding adult time while we're fake dating?"

Travis pulls me into him. "Do you feel how hard I am right now? Walking away from you last night damn near killed me. Hell, yes. Adult time sounds damn good to me."

The elevator opens to our floor. Travis grabs my hand and my lady parts cheer. My heart beats in a rapid rhythmic staccato.

Once the door closes, Travis backs me against the door while his hand trails down my side until he palms my ass. My whimper reverberates through me from the intensity of his stare. "Travis... why aren't you doing anything?"

In a pained voice two octaves lower, Travis says, "Jae, there are so many things that I want to do to you right now. I don't know where I want to start."

I feel my juices trail down my leg. "Pick one." I add in a desperate voice, "*and hurry.*"

Travis leans down and kisses me with a ferocity that sends a heated sensation through my body. Ready for us to be naked... I take off his jacket, then immediately begin pulling his shirt out of his pants. My body moves until my center finds his hard as steel cock. As Travis kisses my neck, I slide up and down finding the friction I need. "Travis..."

He stops and gives me his full attention. "Yes, Jae."

Damn, all thoughts flee. As I struggle to remember, I confess, "I forgot what I was going to say."

Travis drops to his knees and looks up. "Tell me when you remember."

I close my eyes as I feel Travis push my dress above my hips. "Oh, Jae. Damn you're beautiful."

Travis trails kisses from my inner thigh to my hip. Holding my breath as I anticipate his next destination, I'm about to protest when Travis slowly peels down my thong. Eager to get to the good part, I step out of them. When his breath hits my core, he lifts my leg and sets it over his shoulder. The touch of his tongue causes a deep-wrenching moan entrenched from a place never explored. Travis moves his tongue up and down my center as he slides a finger inside me. This feels so good, but when he latches onto my clit and sucks hard… I see stars.

As he spreads me wider and flicks his tongue in a rapid up and down motion that makes me tremble, I move against his face. My climax builds. Already the best sex that I have ever had and we haven't even gotten to the good part. I hear Travis, faintly over the keenness that continues to build, say, "Yes, Jae, show me how this feels to you."

My sex feels sensitive, responding to everything. My climax starts to build. "Feels good, so good. I'm close Travis."

Travis feasts on me like he has something to prove. I can't hold back anymore. "Travis… yessssss!"

My climax rams through me like a freight train. Coming harder than I have ever before.

Travis

Carrying Jacqui to my room, I can't wait to be inside her. My need clawing to the surface like a diver running low on oxygen and trying to breach the water. I lie her down, lift off her dress, and remove her bra. Jacqui in 3D beats any fantasy I've had over the years. Her luscious breasts, trim waist and flared hips lie before me like an offering at the altar… Damn. I reverently move my hand from her waist to her breast, trying to hide the tremble.

Unable to wait another minute, my mouth sucks on her hardened nipple while I run my hand down to her clit. She's already come once, but I bet she has one more before we make love. *Make love?* We haven't had sex yet but I know to my core, sex with Jacqui will transcend every experience before her.

One mantra repeats over and over in my head… 'Make her forget every other guy before me.'

Listening to Jacqui's every response as I move to her other nipple, I take hints about what she enjoys. She hums when I rapidly rub my thumb over her clit; and purrs as I insert two fingers and pump into her. When I nibble at the spot on her neck, Jae's movements jerk.

Jae rides my hand pumping faster. Her sex begins to spasm around my fingers. "Travis… don't stop. Don't STOP! I'm commmming!" I continue to stroke her with my fingers as her climax peaks.

The satisfied look on her face makes me want to beat my chest. The satisfied look turns into a pout as she says, "You have on too many clothes."

Smiling, I say, "Not for long." When I'm naked and about to put on the condom, Jae grabs me. Pumping me in her hand a few times before I need to pull back. In a voice that shows my desperation, I say, "Babe, you have to… I don't want to come by your hand. I have other plans for you."

"You do? What's taking you so…"

After handling the condom, I position my head at her entrance and push in slowly. I wasn't sure when was her last time and I didn't want to hurt Jae. After entering about an inch, we both release a satisfied sigh. She feels so tight. Sliding in a little more each time until I'm balls deep, I pause, needing a minute. I don't want this to be over before it even starts. "Damn, Jae. You feel so good. So damn good. Just give me a minute."

Jae moves her hands over my back and down my arms. With an earnest look, Jae exclaims. "Travis, I need you to move now."

"Hold on, baby." To open her wider for me, I hook Jacqui's leg over my arm and feel myself slide even deeper as Jae shivers. Thrusting in and out, over and over, as I work to erase every guy that came before me. My plan is simple: make love to her all night long.

We move together like this isn't our first time. Damn, I'm close, but Jae is first... always first. I reach between us and rub her clit as I say, "I think you have one more in you."

Jae squeezes tighter around my cock as her climax erupts. "Travis, I... oh... right theeeerrrree!"

Her climax triggers mine. "Jae, I'm coming. Oh, fuck." My heart pounds hard. I need a minute to just be in the moment. Jesus. Jae rocked to my core. "Nothing... no one... has ever felt this good." Never wanting to leave the warm cocoon of Jae's body, I reluctantly give Jae a quick kiss before gently getting up to deal with the condom.

On my walk back to the bed, Jacqui appears to be falling asleep. "You're not falling asleep on me, are you, Jae?"

The sated look on her face gives me a clue. "Travis, I'm not ashamed to say—you wore me out."

I chuckle as I pull her closer. "You don't say. Well, you wake me when you're ready for round two. I'm not done with you."

Chapter Seven

Jacqui

Slowly I begin to wake and realize Travis holds me tight in his arms. Who knew? Travis—a cuddler. With his hard chest and eight-pack abs against my back, I feel treasured. I should have known—Travis does nothing half assed. Not tasting him last night, I quietly move down and take my first lick as I wrap my hand around his blessed-with-more-than-his-fair-share cock.

Gliding my mouth over his cock, I can't help the hum that escapes. I take as much of Travis as I can before pulling back. Travis smooths his hand over the back of my neck. He slightly rocks back and forth but doesn't push too hard, letting me set the pace.

In a voice laced with reverence, Travis says. "Jae, your mouth feels like a dream."

Licking from the base to the head before I suck so hard that my cheeks hollow. Travis must like what I'm doing. He says my name like a prayer, so I do it again and again. Before I can finish, Travis lifts me up and kisses me deep.

The sound of Travis trying to open the condom pierces through the silence in the room. Impatient to get to the good stuff, I help him with the condom, slide all the way down, and purr, "Yessss."

Travis lifts me up and down effortlessly while I strum my clit as he holds my hips. The pace drives us out of our mind. "Travis, don't stop. I'm close... so close. Yes, just like that." I careen over a cliff in a million little pieces.

Travis

Seeing Jacqui lose herself triggers my release. My release goes on and on. A myriad of emotions passes through me. One, the sex is off the charts with Jae. Two, I realize I was right—no one compares to Jae. Our time together only confirms what I already knew. Three, I have absolutely no idea how I will walk away from Jacqui when our time is up.

Jacqui falls forward on my chest while I rub from her ass to her neck in slow, rhythmic, up and down movements. Her curves drive me insane and the way her ass feels in my hands, she feels like she's made for me. Jae curls into me, about to doze off. I whisper in her ear, "Jae, babe, let me take care of the condom before you fall asleep. I'll be right back."

While walking back to the bed, I check the time. It's only six thirty in the morning. We can order room service and eat before heading to the airport. Now that I've set the alarm for nine, I pull Jae back into my arms as I enjoy having her in my arms. Knowing we may not have another opportunity for a while, I cherish this moment. With her head under my chin, her strawberry scents wafts lightly as I take a satisfied deep breath.

Being able to take Jae on a date last night and get to know her better over this weekend exceeded my expectations. After heading off to college, I did everything in my power to put Jae out of mind. I thought that I'd done a good job until Jeremy called off the wedding. Knowing she was available, something inside me cracked open. With the possibility of being with Jae dangling like a forbidden fruit, I lost countless hours of sleep. A future I dared to not dream consumed my thoughts. The hardest part, figuring how to overcome the impenetrable wall. This fake relationship opened the door.

The alarm startles me at nine. I turn off the offending noise, realizing that I must have fallen back to sleep. Jacqui turns on her back to face me with a well-fucked look on her face. "Hey, did you sleep well?"

The smile on Jae's face widens as she says lightly, "Yeah, apparently all I needed was great sex. Who knew?"

I chuckle. "Same here. I never sleep past six, but apparently the best sex of my life will do it."

The disbelief apparent as Jae looks at me like an unsolvable Rubik's cube. "Really, Travis. I'm the best sex that you ever had?"

Jae needs to understand I will always be honest with her. May as well start now. "Absolutely. I wouldn't lie to you. We'd be having round three right now if I didn't think you needed a break."

Jae blushes. "Well, you're right. My lady parts got a good workout."

Before Jae can climb out of bed, I pull her into my embrace and give her a something-to-hold-you-over kiss. Shit, who am I kidding? This kiss must give me sustenance until I see her again.

Jacqui

We're thirty minutes outside of Houston when my mom calls. We spoke before the plane departed New York. Something must be wrong. "Mom, everything okay?"

"Everything is wonderful. Gabi has gone into labor. We're on our way to the hospital now. After calling CJ, I tried to call Travis, but the call went straight to voicemail."

Not touching that comment, since Travis is sitting right next to me, I say, "I thought that the doctor wanted to hold off on the delivery for another four weeks. Will the babies be, okay?"

"Sweetie, twins normally come early. You and Jake came around the same time at thirty-six weeks. Don't worry. Everything will be fine. I know that you're flying back. Come to the hospital when you can. The babies may not appear for several hours. I'll try Travis again in about thirty minutes."

"Thanks mom." I turn and give Travis the update. "Oh, and my mom mentioned she was going to try calling you again in about thirty minutes."

Drumming my fingers on the captain's chair, my impatience apparent. Can't we get there any faster? Travis laces my fingers with his. "Jae, don't worry. Everything is going to be fine. We'll get to the hospital soon."

In full panic mode, I begin trying to work through how the hell am I going to get to the hospital. My worry removes any coherent thoughts. "How are we going to do this? We can't show up at the hospital together."

Travis soothes my rattled nerves as he strokes his other hand over our joined hands. "My driver can take me home so I can drop off our luggage and grab my car. Have your driver head directly to the hospital."

My heart pounds thinking of Jake. I should be with him. "Yeah, that works. I can swing by after work tomorrow to pick up my luggage." Travis presence calms me down. Wow, who knew? I have no time to unpack this revelation... later... much later.

As we walk down the stairs of the plane, Travis's phone rings and I hear him say, "Hi, Momma Mac... So sorry that I wasn't available earlier.

I had my phone turned off. Is everything okay? Oh, the girls are ready to make their appearance? I'll be there... Yes, probably in between thirty and forty minutes. Do you need me to bring anything? Okay, I'll see you there."

Travis walks toward me and grabs my hand before I can get in the car. He lifts my chin as he bends for a kiss. I open for him and wrap my arms around his neck. He kisses me like he wants to remind me how good we were together this weekend.

When he pulls back, he's still holding me close. "Jae, I had a great time this weekend."

Unable to pass the opportunity to give Travis a hard time, I smile and joke, "I know you had a great time. I was there, remember?"

Travis looks down and shakes his head like he really doesn't know what to do with me. "Well, yes, that was better than great, but I'm talking about the art show and our dinner date. Thanks for asking me to tag along."

Before I slide into the car, I lean into Travis loving the feel of my body against his. His grip on my waist tightens sending a delicious hum through my body. "Thanks Travis. You're the best fake boyfriend that I've ever had."

He chuckles. "Jae, you're incorrigible. Love seeing this side of you." He gives me a quick kiss. "I'll see you there."

The family waiting room, where we previously waited, contains both dads. The apprehension and excitement permeate through the room. Hard to believe we were all here just last Wednesday. "Dad, I got here as fast as I could."

"Hi, pumpkin. Your mom and Giselle just went back to the room. We should hopefully receive an update soon. How was New York?"

I blush. Why am I blushing? Ding Ding Ding, I know the answer for five hundred Alex—Travis rocked my world. "It was wonderful, dad. Brittney and her parents say hello. Glad the twins weren't born while I was out of town."

CJ walks into the room, giving me an excuse to walk away from my dad while I work to get my nerves under control. "CJ, have you seen Jake yet? I feel bad that I was out of town. I should have been here."

"Jake's got this. His entire world is in that room. Try not to worry. We have the simple part. We just need to wait for the updates. Do you need anything?"

"Coffee sounds divine right now. I saw a coffee shop in the lobby. Let me go with you."

"Jacqui, I've got it." CJ confirms the orders and heads out on the errand.

While sitting next to dad as he talks to Gabi's father, I think back to my weekend with Travis. He shocked me several times this weekend. His attentiveness caught me by surprise. I've always considered Travis as self-absorbed and looking for his next female conquest. Travis never once looked at another woman. This stunned me more than anything. I half expected him to only be on his best behavior when duty called. Even Emma's assistant stated we made a cute couple.

CJ returns with our coffees bringing me out of my reflection. "Thanks CJ. I really needed this. My maid of honor duties wiped me out this weekend. With only four more weeks to go, I'll be able to go back to my routine. How have you been since the baby shower?"

"Good. Travis bailed on me this weekend, so I ran ten miles and swam five to stay on track with our triathlon training. We gave Jake a pass as soon as soon as he shared Gabi was expecting. Man, I can't believe Jake is going to be, not only a dad, but a twin-girl dad. The girls are going to have him wrapped around their fingers."

Smiling, I can see Jake sitting proudly in the front row of their ballet recitals. Jake's life changes tonight. I'm happy for him and Gabi. They love each other so much. The girls will be a great addition. "You're right, CJ. Between Gabi, Samantha and me, we'll make sure Jake understands what the girls need from him."

The atmosphere changed—looking for the source, I casually turn and confirm Travis walked into the waiting room. My nipples bead at the exact moment his gaze finds mine. He walks over to CJ and me. My anxiety skyrockets tenfold but I work to shake off my nerves. No one knows Travis and I spent the weekend getting to know each other *better*. Travis asks, "Any news?"

I shake my head side to side and say, "No, none. We may have a long night."

Travis drags his gaze away from me after a beat and looks at CJ. He appears to be having the same problem. We better get it together before CJ picks up on the sexual energy pinging between us. "I called my boss on the way to give him a heads up to expect me in the office after lunch tomorrow."

Rattled by Travis's presence, I can't remember how I used to act before Travis and I started having adult naked time. CJ jumps in. "I did the same. I let my team know that my schedule would be fluid tomorrow." CJ nudges Travis. "Benefits of being the owner of the company."

This must be an old teasing quip by CJ because Travis nods his head up and down like they have had this conversation a number of times. "Yeah, yeah. I plan to get there one day... just not right now."

Before I add some commentary, the moms walk into the room. Momma G starts, "Gabi received an epidural and dilated to six centimeters. She's as comfortable as she can be until she delivers. The girls' heartbeats are strong. Did I forget anything, Christine?"

"No, Gisselle. I think the only thing that I would add is G and I setup the room like Gabi wanted. We let the kids know that we're going to give them privacy for the birth, but we're here if they need us."

Relieved, I exhale. "Ok, yes, definitely good news. Glad you both spent time with them. Do y'all need anything? CJ grabbed us some coffee, but I don't mind getting you something." Both moms declined. A huge yawn surprises me. From a combination lack of sleep, the best sex of my life and not knowing how to act normal around Travis, I'm rattled. "My New York trip, packed with endless activities, left me pretty tired... better sit before I drop." When I get rattled, I ramble like I'm doing now. Travis coughs in his hand. I'd roll my eyes, but even this feels like too much effort. "I'll just sit back and shut my eyes a bit. Something tells me we may be here a while."

Travis

Occasionally, watching Jacqui as I talk to CJ, I notice she appears to be cold. I excuse myself, go to the nurse's station and bring a warm blanket to cover her. CJ lifts his eyebrow but says nothing. I don't have a plausible explanation, so I turn my back to Jacqui before I give myself away.

After four hours past, we take shifts to grab something to eat. More time passes, I casually glance at my watch... it's already ten o'clock at night. Looks like the babies want a grand entrance. At some point I fell asleep because I wake to Jake stating he has an announcement. After looking at the wall clock, four thirty in the morning projects from the black and red display.

We all stand, feeding off Jake's excitement. Jake starts with a goofy smile, "Gabi is doing great. She's tired, but she's good. The girls were born at three forty-five, weigh five pounds twelve ounces and measure eighteen inches long each. Oh, they took the girls to finish recording their vitals. I can take you to the window if you follow me."

We walk to the nursery talking over each other. We ooh and aah as we see the girls. The moms cry as the dads' clap Jake's back. If the hospital didn't have a no smoking policy, the cigars being passed around would have been lit.

After thirty minutes, we confirm Jake has what he needs and promise to visit later today. As we head out, Jacqui's mom says, "Jacqui, we can take you home."

Before Jacqui can protest, I chime in, "Momma Mac, y'all head home. I pass Jacqui's house on my way home. I'll drop her off."

Momma Mac pats my check and says, "You're a good boy, Travis. Always have been."

I must need more sleep... I swear I choke up.

Jacqui kisses her mom and dad. CJ pulls me in for a man hug while asking in a low voice, "You got this man?"

CJ and I exchange some unspoken dialogue before I say, "Yeah, I got this." The look he gives me confirms CJ plans to discuss this with me sometime soon when we're alone.

As I'm about to place my hand on Jacqui's lower back, I catch myself. After having the weekend where I could touch her freely, I need to be careful when we're around family and friends. Now that I know how she feels, I want to touch her every opportunity that I can. Clearing my throat, I wave my hand to the right. "I'm parked over here."

Chapter Eight

Jacqui

The past twenty-four hours have been a whirlwind. My emotions range from exhaustion to elation—I'm a twin aunt. My nieces have a head full of curly black hair. One sucked her fist while the other one looked around watching all of the commotion. The elation I feel settles over me like a comfy blanket. Ready for my aunt duties to start now, I plan to check with Gabi and the moms to see where I can help.

Travis looks over with a slight smile. "How are you feeling, Auntie Jae? I didn't even ask. Have you decided what you want the girls to call you?"

"I like Auntie Jae, actually. I hope it's easy for the girls to say. How about you?"

Travis shrugs. "I don't know. What do you think, Uncle Travis or Uncle Trav?"

Either name would work but I decide to test my theory. "Yeah, either of those works. Don't be surprised if the girls give you a nickname, like Bubba or Butch."

He looks straight ahead, not focusing on anything, with a dopey smile before answering. "I'm good with whatever they want to call me."

My theory confirmed. I snap my fingers and point at him from my seat. In a sing song voice, I say, "Oh oh, you're head over heels in love with the girls already, too. Aren't you?" I shake my head. "There's zero chance that these girls aren't going to be spoiled rotten."

With a self-deprecating expression, he turns his head towards me. "What can I say that won't incriminate me?"

I pat his cheek like my mom did earlier tonight. "It's okay Uncle Trav. Your secret is safe with me."

We arrived at my house in record time. Amazing how fast you get through town with zero traffic. "Travis, would you like to come in?"

His voice deepens and his eyes smolder. "I'd love to come... in."

I laugh, "You're so bad. Come on, lover boy."

After turning off the alarm, I head straight for the coffeemaker and tiptoe to grab some mugs. Travis places his hand on my waist and reaches above me to pull them down. I tremble and spin right into a kiss that I've wanted since he walked into the waiting room at the hospital.

Our tongues duel as I wrap my arms around him and try to get closer. Travis's kisses drive me wild. My desire ramps as I nip his lip and smooth with my tongue. Got to get Travis naked... I pull off his Henley and bite my lower lip as I take in his broad shoulders and waist that narrow into a delicious V.

My lips touch his chest and my tongue moves in circles around his nipple as I take light nips. Never being this bold before. This new inner temptress wants everything that Travis offers.

Travis removes my clothes and lifts me onto the counter. When he sucks my hardened nipple in his mouth, I feel my juices pool as I unzip Travis's pants and wrap my hand around his hard-as-granite cock. When Travis slides his finger into me and uses my juices to strum my clit, I feel a delicious sensation move up my spine. "That... feels... soooooooo... good, Travis."

Travis looks down mesmerized by how his finger moves in and out... in and out. Grayish blue eyes the color of a developing summer storm seize mine. "Jacqui, come for me... give me one."

When he kisses my neck as he rapidly flicks my clit, my climax barrels through me. "I'm commmminng." My climax goes on and on. I rest my forehead on Travis's shoulder to catch my breath. "You know you're brilliant at this."

Travis

"I could same thing about you. You have me ready to burst." I pull back, grab a condom from my wallet, and suit up in record time. I reach for Jacqui, bringing her to the edge of the counter and plunge into her, unable to hold back any longer.

Jae wraps her legs around my waist; as I stroke into her long and slow... back and forth... back and forth. Sweat runs downs my face and back as I reach between us to rub Jacqui's clit. I just had Jae this morning, but it feels like forever since I've been inside her.

At this angle, I find Jae's distended nipple ready for my attention. My eager tongue pulls Jae's nipple into my mouth. I lean back and blow while taking my time. While continuing to stroke her clit, I move to her other nipple. Jae tightens around me as we work toward her climax.

"Right there. Yes, right there."

"Jacqui, you feel so good. So tight. Are you close?"

"Yes, Travis. I'm close."

My move hits her g-spot... she careens. I feel my release from the base of spine as it travels through my body like a bullet train. "Jacqui. Daaaammmmmnnn!" I slow my movements down as we both come back to earth. The kiss I give Jacqui contains so much emotion I don't have time to unpack what I'm feeling at this moment.

We both look down at the same time and laugh. My pants are down around my ankles. Jacqui huffs and says, "I guess we were in a hurry. You didn't even take off your shoes."

I smile. "Well, I had more important things to do. Here, one second. Ok, little lady. Let's get you down from up there."

Jacqui

Gabi and the girls have been home for almost a week. The girls already look different, giving us a clue how they will look as they continue to grow. Jake and Gabi held off on naming them until they had time to see their personalities.

Harper Gisselle observes the world around her. Hayden Christine waits patiently for her turn. Each girl carries their grandmother's first name as their middle name. I think proudly my nieces will change the world someday.

My phone rings as I turn onto my street. Travis's name appears on the caller ID.

"Hey. Have you eaten?" asks Travis.

"Hey, yourself and no, I have not. What did you have in mind?"

"I know you like the new ramen spot not too far from your house. Feel like company? I can grab a few bowls before heading over."

I giggle. "Now, Travis, if you keep this up, I'm going to think that you like my company."

"Well, I figure the more time we spend together, I'll be better prepared when I meet your friends at the wedding."

I'm a little disappointed, but Travis is right. We're in a fake relationship after all, but we need to make it look real to everyone else. I need to remember this. Travis apparently understands the assignment.

"Favorite dish?" Travis questions.

Maintaining a playful tone, I say, "I'm feeling adventurous. How about you surprise me?"

"Seems I'm rubbing off on you... I like it. See you in an hour."

We catch up on our week and the girls coming home. Not the first time that I noticed Travis and I ease comfortably from one topic to another. Surprised that I genuinely like him as a person and laugh at his self-deprecating stories about his city soccer games. All these years, I considered Travis a bad frat boy, breaking women's hearts all over Houston. Have I been wrong?

"Jacqui, you've been going on and on about *Below Deck*. I'm not convinced."

Playfully, I say, "I'm offended, Travis Prescott. How dare you disparage my choice in shows? I watch the entire *Below Deck* franchise. Few people know this is my guilty pleasure, so you should feel honored." I pause and think about which show to show Travis. "You might like *Below Deck Adventure* best, though. The guests like to go on thrill-seeking activities like para gliding and cave dives."

After giving Travis a crash course on who's who from the deckhands and stew teams, we settle in watching a few episodes. Before long, the antics of the guests and crew pull Travis all the way in. He agrees with me that Captain Kerry needs to be a leader. He's allowing the teams to manage themselves, but communications are breaking down.

I must have fallen asleep because I feel Travis lay me down in my bed. When he stands, I grab his wrist and whisper, "Stay."

Travis looks pained, but he asks, "Are you sure? You've been going non-stop between work and your other commitments."

"Travis, I want you to stay." To prove my intentions, I sit up and kiss his jaw and neck before moving to his mouth as I unbutton his shirt.

Travis

Jacqui helps me remove my shirt as I place my knee on her bed. Just feeling her hands on my chest, my dick goes from a semi to rock hard. I realize at this moment I won't ever tire of Jacqui.

Pulling off Jacqui's t-shirt and shorts to find a beautiful front-clasp light purple bra. I bend and kiss the top of her left breast as Jae releases a slow breath. My hand trails to the top of her underwear and dips inside to find her ready for me.

"Jae, you're soaking wet," I say as I tremble. Trailing kisses down her stomach, I remove her underwear. Not stopping until I'm kneeling on the floor, I pull Jacqui to the edge of the bed. I've been fantasizing about having her like this. I stiffen my tongue and flick her clit rapidly while I pump a finger, then two, into her. Jae rides my hand with wild abandon.

"Travis, yes. Oh... oh."

A man on a mission, I eat Jacqui like she's my favorite dessert alternating between plunging my tongue and flicking her clit in rapid successions. After several rounds, I latch onto Jacqui's clit and suck... hard. She goes sailing.

"Yessssss, Travis!"

Her climax goes on and on. Seeing her let go undoes me... She looks at me and crooks her finger. Standing, I lift Jae and place her in the middle of the bed, then remove my pants lightning quick. As I grab the condom, Jacqui takes it from my hand.

"Not so fast!" As Jacqui holds my cock in her hand, I watch in awe when she leans forward and takes me in her mouth.

My groan comes deep from my core. Nothing feels as good as her mouth. She licks off the pre-cum before taking as much of me as she can in her mouth. When she sucks hard as she moves back to my head, twirls her tongue and begins the torturous trip back down my cock, my eyes roll back in my head. "Jae, your mouth feels amazing."

Slightly pumping a few times, I realize I need to stop before I can't. Pulling back, Jacqui stops my actions and sucks harder. "Baby, that feels so good, but I'm... I cannot hold... back." Jacqui pulls up a little before taking me all the way until I feel the back of her throat. "Jacqui... I'm about to come. Pull up NOW." Jacqui stubbornly continues. I lose the battle and come as Jacqui gently massages my balls.

"Come here, Jae." I have no words but give her a hard kiss and lay down as I place her head on my shoulder while I try to catch my breath. "Jae, I... you... I have no words."

Head tilted slightly with a shocked look, Jae jokes. "You, Travis? I'll have to make a note for future reference."

"You do that."

෮ᓚ♡ᓗ෮

We both slept through the night, holding each other. I've never been one for regular overnights, but with Jacqui, I'm finding it difficult to sleep without her. Jae wiggles her ass as she snuggles into the pillow. Problem, my morning wood makes his presence known. Stifling a groan, I plan to wait patiently until Jae wakes up.

When Jae wiggles again and giggles, thank God... she's up. Throughout the night, I held her breast in my palm. Now, I give it a squeeze. Moving to kiss her shoulder, then the back of her ear, I love the answering purr that emanates from her mouth. "I'm glad that you're up."

"Hmmm, I can tell."

Trailing my hand down from her side to her front to discover she's soaking wet. When I add a second finger, Jacqui moves as I pump.

"Travis, this feels... this feels decadent."

Finding the condom that I placed on the nightstand; I regretfully pull my fingers from her heated core. The need to get on this condom before we both get caught up in the moment presses down on me with urgency. My hands tremble as I rip the foil packet open and roll it down on my straining cock.

Lifting her leg, I enter from behind. My strokes slow and deep. I reach around and begin strumming Jacqui's clit. Just when I think Jacqui can't get any wetter, she surprises me. Wet sounds surround us as Jae soaks my cock. "Jacqui, you feel amazing, baby. I will not last much longer. Are you close?"

"Yes, Travis... so close."

My other hand circles her hardened nipple while I continue to give her clit attention. Her climax rolls through her. My strokes pump into her faster with short, rapid succession. My climax starts at the base of my spine and rams through me like a meteor.

We both work to catch our breath. Hands down... no one compares to Jacqui. I mean... then I pause. No, no correction needed. No other woman is in the same stratosphere. My deliberation stutters as I conclude I think I'm falling in love with Jacqui, but how would I know? I've never been in love.

Jae breaks through my thoughts. "Are you falling asleep, Travis?"

Kissing her neck, I try to come up with an excuse. "No... just thinking about breakfast. Do you have ingredients to make an omelet?"

Jacqui

Travis continues to amaze me. He spent a night and now he's making me breakfast. "Where did you learn to cook?"

"While at Yale Law, I moved to this complex for graduate students. One of my classmates married a chef who opened a restaurant near campus. He took pity on me and showed me a few dishes."

The low-riding pajama bottoms sit on Travis's hips giving me a front row seat to all of his deliciousness. My mouth waters as I sit perched on my bar stool. His shirtless muscular back on full display when he turns to check on the food on the stove. "What are your favorite dishes to make?"

He answers without hesitation. "Hands down... chicken parm, then a close second is chicken piccata."

"Why am I not surprised? Your grandmother is Italian, correct?"

"Yeah, but it's been years since I've seen her. My mom and grandmother had a falling out. My mom never told me the entire story, but it had something to do with my dad."

Sadness for the lost time he will never get back, I fight to find the right words. "Oh, Travis, that's so sad. I don't know what I would do without my grandma. Our conversations keep me sane. I've been able to share with her the struggle that I'm having around chasing my dream or continuing to work at the firm. Where is your grandma now?"

Travis shrugs his shoulders like the absence doesn't hurt, but his eyes tell a different story. He misses his grandmother. "She moved back to Italy after my grandfather passed. I can't remember the last time that I spoke to her."

Travis pauses a moment. I give him time to collect his thoughts.

"Jae, talking with you makes me realize I need to call my grandmother. I've been busy, you know... first, finishing law school and studying for the bar... then, working to establish a name for myself at my company. Whatever the reason, these aren't good excuses why I haven't called. I just hope she will want to speak to me."

He told me a few weeks ago he would be there for me if I needed him when I talk to my parents. I want to offer him the same but Travis reminded me our fake relationship has an expiration date. Instead, I decide to give him the encouragement he gave me. "She will. I bet she will surprise you and be over the moon to hear from you."

Travis plates our omelets while I place the coffee, buttered toast, and jam on the table. This feels very domesticated. Not the first time I realize, my impressions of Travis may not be accurate. I've always considered him to be standoffish and heartless, not this open, easy-to-talk-to guy.

Pulled from my reflection, I lift my head to see Travis slather jam on his toast as he asks. "What do you plan to do today before the gala?"

"I started a new painting I plan to continue to work on today, then I'll probably spend some time with Jake, Gabi and the girls early this afternoon."

He places his elbow on the table as he takes a sip of his coffee. The smile on Travis's face genuine. "Fatherhood fits Jake. I saw them earlier this week and plan to stop by on Monday after work. Jake and Gabi deserve all the happiness." Travis shakes his head before continuing. "Still can't believe he went from a bona fide bachelor to finding the love of his life, getting married and now kids, all in less than two years."

Curiosity piques my interest leading me to ask, "What about you? Have you ever thought about a wife and kids?"

"Honestly, after having a front-row seat to my parents' catastrophe of a marriage, I wanted none of it."

Travis practically stayed at our house when we were in high school leaving me to believe his home life wasn't ideal. Jake shared pieces of information occasionally but I never wanted to pry. "I get that Travis. With Jeremy's betrayal, I felt like I broke into a million pieces. Now doing the work to pull myself together, some days take everything that I have to make it through the day."

Travis looks perplexed and shows genuine concern. "In what way?"

Surprised I am about to share something with Travis Jake doesn't know. I pause for a moment to gather the courage to continue. "Believe it or not, the benign question '*How are things going?*' causes me to stumble when I'm not having a good day. It takes everything that I have to paste on a smile and say, '*things are good. How are you?*' When I'd rather say, '*today isn't a good day for me*' but we both know the truth makes folks uncomfortable."

The pained look on Travis's face confirms he understands. "Jae, I'm so sorry that you've been going through this alone. I know this hasn't always been the case, but you can always reach out to me. You don't have to pretend with me."

I lean over my chair and kiss Travis on the cheek. "Thanks for that, Travis. Means more to me than I can say."

We finish breakfast, and before I can rise to clean up, Travis stands. "Let me, Jae. Get ready for the day. I'll clean up and be out of your hair when I'm done."

Chapter Nine

Jacqui

After Travis left this morning, I feel damn near giddy. Sex with Travis eclipses any of my other partners. The old adage 'practice makes perfect' definitely applies in Travis's case. Probably in poor taste, but I want to send those girls a thank you note and maybe some flowers. Travis expects what I need before I even know. I shiver deliciously thinking about that thing that he did with tongue as he feasted on me.

Shaking off the memory, I focus on getting ready for the MD Anderson Christmas Gala. This year was the first time I joined a committee... choosing to volunteer as an elf, passing out gifts to the kids on the cancer wing of the Children's Hospital. Seeing the kids' faces illuminate as we walked into their room made all of my issues slip away. Next year, I want to be more involved.

Keeping Travis in mind when deciding what to wear tonight sends delicious wicked shivers through my body. A quick stop to my waxing goddess has me plunked in all the right places. My hairstylist added a volumizer and beach waves to my hair, cascading my hair over one shoulder.

Deciding on the side where I wanted my hair pulled was easy. I chose the side that would ensure that my bare shoulder would be on full display. The black Dior off-the-shoulder embellished gown makes me feel like a vixen. With the La Perla black strapless bra and matching lace thong, Travis won't know what hit him.

This year's gala, *Noel Noir: A Silver and Black Christmas Soiree*, feels like old Hollywood elegance. The ten-member orchestra plays *My Favorite Things* as I pass under a silver and black balloon arch with glitter and shiny balloons in different sizes. A waiter offers me a glass of champagne as I look for my parents.

I find my parents talking to members of the board. My mom looks gorgeous tonight in her black Valentino gown. I kiss mom as I sing, "Mom, you look marvelous."

Off to my right, my dad says, "Hey, what am I, chopped liver?"

Playfully, I roll my eyes. "Dad, that's so lame. No one says things like that anymore and no, you're actually the most handsome man here tonight," I say as I give him a kiss on the cheek.

My dad's eyes twinkle as he adds, "Now, you're talking."

"Sweetie, did you come by yourself?" asks my mom with some concern in her voice.

"Yes, mom, but I don't want you to worry."

"It's my job to worry."

Changing the subject before my mom can say something about setting me up with one of the board members' sons, I go with giving my mom praise on the gala. "Mom, love the black and silver décor this year. You and the board do an amazing job each year with this gala. Having it here at the JW Marriott in the Galleria is hands down my favorite location to date."

The twinkle in her eyes shines bright. Mom started volunteering for MD Anderson over ten years ago after my grandfather's bout with cancer. She saw firsthand how hard the doctors and nurses work to provide the highest level of care. My grandfather's cancer went into remission. He faithfully gets his scans once a year and changed his lifestyle by retiring early, eating healthy and exercising regularly. "Thanks so much for your help with distributing gifts at the Children's hospital. We've already heard from many of the parents how much the kids loved seeing Santa and the elves."

My mom subtlety tries to get me to mingle in hopes I'll meet someone here by encouraging me to walk around. Fine with not looking for Mr. Right... Mr. Right Now, works and lucky for me, Travis fits the bill. A sex god, laid back, and funny make him the perfect candidate. Not sure when I'll be ready to jump back into the dating pool, my current arrangement meets my needs.

Looking for anyone as I walk always from my parents, I'm relieved to see Marianne from accounting. We try to grab lunch at least once a month. To ensure I don't smudge our makeup, I grab her hands and give her air kisses on each side. "Marianne, glad to see you here. How was your Thanksgiving?"

"It was good. How was yours? Do anything special?"

Feeling the atmosphere change around me, I look around for the source. Of course, Travis. He heads toward me. Boy, that man knows how to wear a tuxedo. He looks like Chris Hemsworth, with brown hair and smoldering eyes that make me squirm with their focused concentration.

Travis

With Jake and Jacqui's mom chairing the charity event, I make a point of attending each year. Knowing the proceeds go to cancer research is a bonus. The server approaches to offer a champagne-filled glass at the exact time I see Jacqui talking to a coworker from her dad's architectural firm. She looks drop-dead gorgeous in the off-the-shoulder black full-length gown. She's done something different with her hair... pulled to the side, leaving her beautiful neck and shoulder on display. I had my hands and mouth all over her last night.

Like a programmed torpedo, I walk straight toward her. On autopilot, I bend to kiss her check when she subtly steps back with a slight shake of her head. Damn, I lost my head for a second. Jacqui and I do not greet each other with a kiss on the cheek. I play it off and try not to show my regret.

Extending my hand instead. "Hey Jacqui, good seeing you here. How have you been?" The blush that rises on her face intrigues me. With a lift of my eyebrow, I wonder what she's remembering. We did a few things last night that would make her blush.

She answers after introducing Marianne and me. "I've been good. Spoke to Jake on the way over. Gabi and the girls are doing well. I plan to head over tomorrow to give them an opportunity to nap while I watch my nieces. He shared both moms have been taking turns as well."

She gives me an update she knows isn't news, but we have an audience and need to pretend like we talk occasionally. "I'll check with Jake to see if he needs anything. I'm not up for diaper duty, but I'm pretty sure there are plenty of things to do where he could use an extra pair of hands. It was good catching up. Take care." Only wanting to stay here and be with Jacqui, I'd actually like to hold her against my side and maybe have a few turns on the dance floor. With great effort, I turn to walk away and feel like someone just took the one thing that I love in the world away from me.

CJ walks in my direction with two bourbons. Happily sitting the champagne down, I needed something stronger, especially after having to walk away from Jacqui. "Thanks man. I needed this more than you know."

CJ tilts his head. "Really? Is everything ok? I saw you talking to Jae. How is Jake doing with his girls?"

He knows me better than Jake. Best to keep him distracted before he looks closer into what could be wrong with me. "They're doing well. Jacqui plans to spend tomorrow watching her nieces so Jake and Gabi can rest. The moms are helping as well, alternating days. I plan to check with Jake to see if he needs anything. Are you solo tonight?"

A conspirator smile appears on CJ's face. "Yeah, I came alone. Guess I'm on what you may call a cleanse of sorts. Now that I plan to explore the chemistry between Samantha and me, I want to make sure that my affairs are in order, so to speak. Not sure if you even understand what I mean."

CJ sounds like he's doing what I did once Jae ended her engagement with Jeremy. No other woman compared. "I think I do... are you saying no other woman is her?"

CJ snaps his fingers and nods. "Yes... that's it exactly. You continue to surprise me, Travis. Come on, I'll be your wingman. Let's see if we can find someone for you tonight."

Not prepared to evade CJ's insistence on finding a random girl tonight, panic rips through me. Going home solo while I wait for Jae to come over afterward is the plan. We agreed to leave thirty minutes apart, a little after ten. "You know, CJ. I actually have to be in the office early tomorrow for a breakfast strategy session. The buyer's lawyers keep throwing up roadblocks."

CJ narrows his eyes like he's trying to figure out what's going on. He scoffs, "Since when has that mattered? You normally ask them to leave by seven in the morning, anyway."

Yeah, he's right. I cringe, not my proudest moment. The disaster called my mom and dad's marriage left me believing love doesn't exist. If it hadn't been for Jake and Jacqui, I wouldn't have known that families were functional. "I'm good, CJ. I see one of my teammates from the soccer team." Rambling, trying to throw CJ off my scent, I continue, "We have a match with The Woodlands intermural team next week. Their forward moves across the field with footwork that makes even my jaw drop. I bet he gets picked up by a USL Division II team. He's just that good. Want to come over with me?"

"Nah man, I'm going to network for a bit and head on home." He claps my back as I move away.

"Joe, good seeing you here. Do you think that we have a chance against The Woodlands next weekend?"

Joe answers truthfully, "This game will be a battle. We'll be lucky to score two goals. If our defense holds, we could win. Competition will be fierce, especially with them having Sebastian—he's a beast. He's been trying out for a few USL teams, according to what I heard. I guess on the bright side, if he gets selected, we won't have to face him anymore. Where have you been, man? You're usually at the Remington Bar on Wednesdays, but I haven't seen you in about a month. How have you been?"

Trying not to give away that a girl... not *a* girl, *the* girl, is the reason for my recent absence from my go to bar, I answer quickly without pausing, "Good, I'm good. Working a deal that's confidential but has been keeping me busier than normal. Randy mentioned we may need to find another place to practice this week. If we do, I have a friend at Rice in the Athletics Department."

"Sounds good. It was good seeing you, Travis. I better run. I see my wife trying to find me in the crowd." Joe heads off toward his wife with a smile on his face that makes me ache for what he has.

What would Jacqui do if I told her I'd like to settle down but not only settle down, but settle down with her? I want what Jake and Joe have... women who they love unconditionally and women who love them. Never dreamed I would be anything but a bachelor. Until now, I never felt jealous of my married friends with families before. I would brag about my freedom to sleep with different women and go on adventures at a moment's notice.

Desperately wanting to walk back over to Jacqui and stake my claim, but I can't... Jae would freak out. Especially since she thinks that this is only a fake relationship with an expiration date. She means the world to me. I need to show her I've loved her since high school, but how? To say my reputation proceeds me is the understatement of the year, probably the decade.

Since I walked away from her, I've been aware of her every move. Trying but failing to tear my eyes away. I need to leave before someone picks up Jacqui has my full attention. Blending with the crowd, I walk heads down to my car, feeling like I'm so far out of my depths right now. I text Jae as I reach my car.

Me: Heading out. Come over whenever you're done. I'll be waiting up.

Jacqui: Is everything ok?

Me: Yeah.

Jacqui's heels click up my driveway. Not waiting until she knocks, I open the door and wrap my arm around her waist as I walk inside backwards and close the door. My kiss welcomes her like I haven't seen her in over a year as I press her against the door. Tongues dueling for dominance. Jae wants me as much as I want her. Nipping her bottom lip, then smoothing my tongue, my hands hold her gently as I continue to kiss her deeply.

I hear a groan, but not sure if it came from me or Jae. "You know this dress drove me out of my mind," Growling, I add, "And your neck, damn Jae. You about brought me to my knees." After dropping a kiss to her jaw, I move to her neck as I leave a trail of heat in the wake.

Jae pants, "Travis, I feel you everywhere. Can't wait. I need you... NOW!"

Having other plans, I drop to my knees. My hands take a slow, torturous path up the back of her legs. When I reach my destination, I pull down her thong then spread her for my eager mouth. So desperate, she's gloriously bare in front of me. What do we have here? "Jae, is this fresh wax just for me?" Not waiting for a response, I latch onto her clit and take a long suck as I hear her whimper.

The pleasure from feasting on Jae rachets my need. She tastes like a delectable treat on my tongue. Bringing her close to her climax, I back off by kissing her thigh. When she pulls my hair, I get the message, but her pleading, "Travis, p-l-e-a-s-e," confirms what she wants.

Dipping inside as she drips on my tongue, I pull back and indulge on her clit as she moves in rhythm with me. My pleasure comes in making her feel good. My dick throbs to be inside her, but not before she comes. Jae jerks and careens as she finds her release. My movements slow as I bring her back down.

Jacqui

As I'm about to return the favor, Travis stands, lifts me in his arms, and walks me to his bedroom. Leaning to nip his earlobe and kiss behind his ear, Travis's grip tightens as he growls, "I'm on the edge, Jae. I need to be in you like five minutes ago."

Sex with Travis... My tingles have tingles, especially now being in Travis's personal space. Travis places me on my feet. Giving him access to my zipper, I turn and pull my hair to the side. I look over my shoulder as Travis concentrates on pulling down the zipper. Cocooned in a Travis bubble. His room smells like him... woodsy and all male. No surprise, his large slate gray Euro-styled king size bed dominates the room.

My dress pools on the floor. I bend to remove my shoes when Travis's voice cuts through the silence in a rough grumble, "Those stay on."

My man needs a release... good, we agree. Smiling, I turn and begin pushing his sweats as I kneel before him. His cock springs out, pointing toward his navel. In a husky whisper, I wrap my hand over his hard as stone cock and slowly move up then down while slightly squeezing. Mesmerized by the movement, I reverently wrap my lips over his head and pull him inside my mouth until I feel him hit the back of my throat. I hum and repeat the process.

My head bobs up and down as I pull all the way up. Swirling my tongue and licking him from base to tip before taking him in my mouth, I switch to a faster rhythm as I hear Travis moan. He lifts me into his arms and kisses me with a desperation I feel pulsing through his body.

"Jae, baby, if I don't get inside you now..."

With more patience than I have, I say with a coy voice, "I'm right her Travis."

Travis moans, kisses me deeply as he walks me backward to his bed. He reaches for his nightstand and grabs a condom. He turns me gently and dons the condom. One hand grips my hip as his other hand glides over my ass to my waist. His callous hands elicit pricks of pleasure as he worships my body. He enters my dripping wet pussy from behind and I eagerly want more. Looking over my shoulder, I see Travis hyper-focused where our bodies are joined with a desire on his face.

Travis is holding back. I don't want him to hold back. "Harder, Travis. I won't break."

"Baby..."

"No, fuck me, Travis."

Travis grabs my hips and moves with fast, long strokes. Repeatedly, but when he bends his knees and tilts my pelvis, I see stars. He hits my g-spot with an accuracy I didn't know was possible. I pant, "Do that again... just like that."

Beads of sweat trickle down his face while he fucks like we have all the time in the world. "You feel so good, Jae, so damn good. I'm close, but you first. You're always first. Take your hand and play with yourself."

Reaching between my legs, I pleasure myself like I do in the privacy of my home. Any shyness that I thought I would have doesn't exist. "Travis, I'm close so close. Don't stop."

"I feel you, baby. Come for me. Now!"

I shatter as my climax hurtles through me.

Travis

Jacqui's intense climax triggers mine. I feel drained and full at the same time. Words I'm not ready to say threaten to burst from my mouth, so I kiss Jae's shoulder, gently disengage, and lay her in the bed. "Baby, just give me a moment. I'll be right back."

Jae appears to be half asleep when I return. I remove her heels, gather her in my arms as I center her in the bed and kiss her temple. "Goodnight, baby."

"Goodnight, Travis."

Chapter Ten

Travis

After making breakfast for Jacqui and me, we talked about the gala as we ate. The gala broke last year's donations record by collecting over two million dollars. Making a mental note, I plan to donate one of my furniture pieces next year.

Jacqui left shortly after ten this morning to head home and continue to work on a new piece for a Spring exhibition. Bailing on CJ, I missed our Sunday training again to be with Jae, and I'm surprised CJ hasn't called me out for missing two Sundays in a row.

Watching the Houston NFL game against Tennessee, I walk to my fridge to grab a beer as I hear my doorbell. Thinking it's Jacqui, I don't even look through the peephole before opening the door. "Oh, hey...." I almost said Jae. Trying not to show my disappointment, I walk away and leave the door open.

CJ walks toward my kitchen to grab a beer as he asks, "Oh, hey? That's the greeting that I get? What's up with you, man? You haven't been yourself lately. First, last night at the gala and then you canceled our run this morning. Did you end up hooking up with a girl, after all?"

Focused on the game, I try to pretend nothing is wrong. But the aggravation in my voice, gives me away when I ask, "CJ, can we just leave it?"

"Normally, I would, but I get the sense that you need to talk to someone."

Turning my head, I slide my eyes to him. "CJ, I don't know. I really don't want to dump this on you."

CJ ponders my statement for a moment. I can tell the moment he decides he's ready for the bombshell I'm about to drop. He takes the lead. "Thinking back over the past few weeks, I know something is up. The first time that I noticed something was off was right after the baby shower. Did something happen after you left the baby shower?"

I stand up and start pacing. "I... I'm not sure..."

CJ looks at me like one of those complex Lego structures he likes to build then a spark of awareness flashes in his eyes. "Does this have anything to do with Jacqui?"

I sputter. "Why... why would you think that?"

"I don't know, but you're different around her. Before, you didn't even notice when she was in the room, but yesterday at the gala, I watched you across the room. You practically tracked every movement she made. Now that I think about, Jacqui was acting weird at Thanksgiving. I casually joked with her if she sat on the opposite end of the room to get as far away from you as possible. She nervously laughed and said *'don't be ridiculous'* but glanced at you briefly."

Trying to figure out what I'm going to say, I stop pacing and sit there. This shouldn't be hard... I'm a lawyer, for Christ's sake. I feel sweat roll down my back as I clear my throat. "Well... here's the thing. I'm sorta seeing Jacqui at the moment."

CJ jumps up and starts to pace. "What do you mean by you're sorta seeing Jacqui at the moment? Shit, man. Have you lost your mind? Jake will kick your ass when he finds out. Hell, I'll kick your ass for him if you hurt her."

Once CJ stops pacing and sits back down, I turn to him. Using my hands to express my sincerity, I speak from the heart. "Believe me, I'll kick my ass if I hurt her. This all has a simple explanation, really."

The look on CJ's face is priceless. He tilts his head and looks at me like I've lost my mind. "Really, please educate me, Travis, because I'm close to kicking your ass now."

"No ass kicking needed; I promise. I'm actually doing a favor for Jae. She needed a plus one for her friend's New Year's Eve wedding. I said yes."

CJ smirks with disbelief. "This can't be all of it. Out with everything, Travis."

"Jae and I have been spending time together. I went with her to New York the weekend after Thanksgiving."

"Jacqui's mom mentioned in passing, when she called me, she was trying to get in touch with you to let you know Gabi had gone into labor."

I nod. "Jacqui and I were together flying back from New York."

CJ lets out a deep breath. I really hate putting him in the middle. CJ, Jake, and I are more like brothers than friends. We've been through every milestone together... the good and the bad. "Man, I don't know what to say. I still feel like I'm missing something. What aren't you telling me?"

I swallow. CJ zeros in on my bobbing Adam's apple, waiting for the next shoe to drop. "I'm pretty sure that I'm catching feelings for Jae."

He jumps up, "Well, stop it! You're going down a path wrought with landmines, man. Do you really want to go down this road?"

"Believe me, CJ, if I could stop it, I would. Even after being with her for any period of time, I want to see her again."

My head rests in my hands. I hear CJ plop down on the sofa and say, "Damn."

There's a sense of heaviness in the room that I can't ignore. Things have gone way past turning back. Even though I'm not sure what's going on, I want to keep seeing Jae after the wedding. I want to see if we can have more than a fake relationship. I want to take Jae on an actual date in our hometown. I have so many wants; it would take me all night to list them.

After my confession, I pretty much shutdown. CJ stayed around until halftime, clapped me on my back and said he would be here if I needed him.

Trying to figure out what I'm going to do about my feelings for Jacqui, I keep hitting a brick wall. Our chemistry is off the charts. We can talk about anything. Deep down, I think that I always knew on some level Jacqui and I were missing puzzle pieces that clicked, but what does this mean? I don't even know how Jae feels. Does she want to be in a relationship so soon after her broken engagement? Would she want to be in a relationship with me?

High school was the last time I was in a relationship with my girlfriend, Kayla. I was the star soccer player, and Kayla was the head cheerleader. Kayla and I both fed into expectations that we should be together. She even stated this when she broke up with me before senior prom. Not giving Kayla a second glance, I went to the senior prom stag and had the time of my life, hooking up with Stephanie before the night was over.

Leaning my head back on the couch, I close my eyes and remember how neither one of my parents took an interest in raising me. My one constant was my nanny, Mildred. At first, I didn't realize that having a nanny take and pick you up from school; take you to your practices; or doctors' appointments weren't normal. My dad worked late hours and traveled constantly, so he was never at home. My mom, now I know she's what you would call a *'woman who lunched.'* Between the country club and her pet projects, she had little to no time for me. She'd show off my accomplishments to her friends when it suited her... a winning goal that I scored or making the honor roll.

In first grade, I looked forward to having cupcakes brought to school for my birthday. At six, I fantasied my mom would walk into the room in a flourish, smoother me with kisses, pass out the cupcakes (knowing all of my friends' names) and stay to the end of school to take me out for my favorite ice cream. In reality, Mildred dropped the cupcakes off in the morning at the office when she dropped me off at school.

Timmy, the class bully, teased me that the teacher had to pass out the cupcakes. I was so mad that I pushed Timmy and hit him in the nose. My mom didn't even bother to come to the school when called. Mildred arrived, took one look at my dirtied white-collar shirt and grass-stained uniform shorts before talking to the principal. I sulked the entire drive home. Mildred gave me time to myself until bedtime. She started reading my favorite book and asked quietly how was I doing. I cried in her arms, not having the words to ask why my parents didn't love me.

Through elementary and middle school, I steeled my emotions and pretended that it didn't matter whether my parents cared to be a part of my life or not. Having Jake and his parents come into my life the first year of high school changed the trajectory. Subtle changes at first. I laughed more. The weight I always carried on my chest seemed to dissipate. I spent more days and nights staying at the McAdams' home than my own. The first two years, Jake, Jacqui and I were like the three musketeers. Jacqui followed Jake and me around on the weekends. We played laser tag, miniature golf, and arcades together. Jacqui played Mortal Kombat with a wicked mean streak. Looking at her, she was tiny, but used the innocent look to her advantage.

How will I look Jake in the eyes? What would Jake say if he knew I was falling in love with his sister? What am I going to do? Jacqui makes me want to be a better man. In the few weeks we have been spending time with each other, I dream of a future together. I forgot how easy it is to talk with Jacqui. She could always help me see another person's point of view when we were younger and nothing has changed.

Jacqui's smiling face when she was teasing me about the tourist Christmas New York pictures (I still have on my phone from my previous visit) flashes in mind. The smirk she gives when she's yanking my chain makes my day every time.

Momma Mac opens the door to Jake and Gabi's house. I bend to kiss her cheek. "Hey Momma Mac. How are my God-daughters treating you?"

Closing the door, we walk into the great room. "Good, they are the most beautiful girls in the world. I'm over the moon and Gabi continues to get stronger with each day. Can you stay for lunch? Nothing complicated, just soup and sandwiches... should be ready in about thirty minutes."

"Sounds delicious. Did you make your famous lobster bisque?" When she nods, I rub my stomach. "Momma Mac, you know a way to a man's heart."

Gabi and Jake walk into the room. When Gabi says, "Hey Travis, good to see you. Thanks for the lovely flower arrangement. Glad that you stopped by." She smiles before adding, "Jake could use some male bonding time."

Jake pulls Gabi to his side and whispers in her ear. Whatever he said makes her blush. She playfully pushes him away. I shake my head. I can only imagine.

Jake gives me our normal complicated handshake we created our sophomore year of varsity soccer in high school. "Hey man, glad you stopped by. Girls just fell asleep. If you stay long enough, you should be able to see them. How does a beer sound? We can head outside while we wait for lunch."

After taking a long draw of my beer, I look over at Jake. "Fatherhood looks good on you, man. How have Gabi and the girls been doing?"

Jake beams with happiness. "They're doing well. Thank God for our moms and dads. Having the extra help with twins has allowed Gabi and me to get the rest we need. Without their help, we would be sleep-deprived zombies. What have you been up to?"

Not sure why, the question conjures Jacqui's face from last night while I was balls deep. I choke and start coughing. I raise my index finger while rasping, "Went down the wrong pipe." Finally, the coughing spell ends. "Working mostly. If everything goes well, the acquisition deal should be signed by February."

Jake shakes his head. "Can't say I miss work. Having the extra time to help Gabi with the girls leaves me feeling equal parts overwhelmed and grateful. I worried myself sick with all the likely scenarios about what could have happened." Jake chuckles. "Mom confided Jacqui called me a mother hen because I was always hovering over Gabi."

I laugh and remember Jacqui telling me the same thing. "Well, I can only imagine. I probably would be the same way. So many things are outside of your control."

Jake nods realizing that I do understand. "Yes, when I thought of all the things outside of my control, I barely slept some nights." Jake looks at me speculatively before continuing, "Do you think you'll ever want to settle down?"

I take a deep breath and think. Deciding to tell him the truth without confessing I want to settle down with Jacqui. "Seeing you with Gabi and now the girls, honestly, makes me wonder."

"Gabi knows me so well. I needed some male bonding time. When both moms and Jacqui are here, I'm outnumbered six to one."

I laugh. "Yeah, I bet that's hard for you. If you ever want to join CJ and me for a drink or a round of golf, let us know."

Shaking his head, *no*, he confirms. "I really don't want to be too far away from the girls right now. Maybe instead, I'll have y'all over to watch a game in the theater room or something."

"Works for me, but only if it doesn't cause extra work for anyone. I can pick up appetizers from Houston's on the way. Name the day."

"Sure, I'll check with Gabi in about a week or two and will let y'all know."

Chapter Eleven

Jacqui

Looking down at my watch, I realize I have less than an hour to get ready. I can only blame myself... I jumped Travis and had my way with him. More than worth being late. Brittney will not appreciate her maid of honor being late though. The more that I think about it, this is actually Travis's fault. He walked around shirtless with his scrumptious body on display and tempted me into another round of explosive sex.

I had to throw him out of our suite so I could get dressed. He kept distracting me with his smoldering eyes. Slammed with a realization, I must sit on the edge of the bed. What the hell? I bring my hand to my mouth and whisper in disbelief, "No, it can't be." It can't be love, maybe strong like for Travis. I don't even like him... let alone what would that look like. He's a man whore personified. I've never known Travis to date for any significant period or to be in a relationship.

After this weekend, Travis and I are supposed to part ways. Would he even be open to continuing whatever-this-is-with-benefits arrangement? We'd have to remain a secret and be very careful that no one finds out, but I'm game if he is. On the flight home tomorrow afternoon, I'll bring up the subject.

After showering, blow drying my hair, and applying my makeup, I step into the rose gold chiffon strapless gown but can't zip it up. As if wishing Travis were here, he walks back into the bedroom of our suite.

I look over my shoulder to see Travis looking at my ass. "Travis, stop that. That's why I'm running late now."

Travis lifts an eyebrow. "Do I need to replay who jumped whom? Not that I'm complaining." He moves toward me slowly, like a cheetah stalking his prey, with a wolfish smile on his face. I've never seen this playful side of Travis. Sexier than when he's having his way with me, I better keep this little secret to myself before he adds this to his sexual arsenal.

"Travis, no, I know that look. We don't have time for any more adult time."

With a Cheshire cat grin, he begins to use his lawyer skills on me. "Adult time... Are you sure? I can be quick."

In a serious voice, I squint my eyes letting him know we don't have time for playtime. "I need you right now, and that's getting me in my dress, *not* out of my dress."

Travis looks so sad that I give a quick kiss on the lips.

"Ok, Jae. You look gorgeous, by the way. Turn around."

Travis does nothing half measure. He slowly zips my dress while dragging his finger as light as a feather up my spine. When I shiver, I turn with accusatory eyes. "You did that on purpose."

Travis steps back with no remorse. "Reminding you of what's coming later."

Travis lets me use him like a chair to steady myself as I put on my glittery rose gold strappy heels. "I'm headed to the bridal suite. Can you be ready in an hour? Once you're done, head to the Terrace Room. Seat yourself on the bride's side."

"Yes, ma'am. If I haven't already told you, I like your bossy side."

I give Travis a deadpan look and say, "Shut up, Travis." He sees my smile before I turn and walk out.

Travis

This weekend officially marks the end of our fake relationship. Maybe my first step should be to tell Jacqui I don't want this to end. Jae and I click. Over the past five weeks, I have had more fun than I can remember. Biggest surprise, my love for Jacqui only continues to grow stronger. I want to take her on a proper date in Houston. Show her I'm not serial-one-night-stand Travis and convince her to take a chance with me. Not normally a patient man, I'm willing to take as much time as Jae needs. The more she shared about Jeremy, only solidified for me he was not the man for her... I am.

Everything went according to plan at the wedding. The entire time, my eyes stayed focused on Jae. Seeing her eyes water as they recited the vows brought a lump to my throat. What I wouldn't give to be exchanging wedding vows with Jae. I want everything... Jake and CJ as my best men; as many bridesmaids as Jae wants, Jae walking toward me on her dad's arm.... the church, the reception. I need to figure out how to tell her I love her.

Jacqui

Words escape me... the wedding felt like a dream. The love between Brittney and Mark was palatable. I tried to keep my tears at bay as they recited their vows, but lost the battle. My resolve deepens... I need to figure out what to do about Travis. He is not the settle down type of guy.

One word… *heartbreak* comes to mind. No, I need to convince my heart to find someone else to love.

I feel someone grab my elbow. "Oh, hi, Danny." After giving him a quick hug, I say, "Brittney said that you would be here. How have you been? Are you still working for the Southern District of New York?"

Danny sticks out his chest with a great sense of achievement. "Yeah, after clerking with Judge Bristol, the cases hooked me. Now, I lead the financial crimes division as senior counsel. Enough about me. How have you been? You know you are the one who got away?"

I cringe, not wanting a walk down memory lane. Danny's a nice guy from an affluent family, but I still feel his clammy hands whenever he would hold my hand. His over-confidence turned me off. He thought his pedigree was all he needed and girls would fall at his feet. Not to mention, we had zero chemistry versus the chemistry between Travis and me sizzles. A hard chest presses against my back… Travis. My body melts into him. He makes me feel like I'm the only woman in the room. What am I going to do? My heart says *take a chance*, but my head says *tread carefully, remember his track record.*

Travis

Walking back with Jae's drink, I notice some guy talking to her once the crowd parts. Jae leans back, trying to create some distance while not being overly obvious. Well, as her boyfriend, fake boyfriend, whatever, I don't like it one bit. I walk up behind Jae; give her the drink and tuck her into my side while giving her a kiss on her temple. "Who's this Jae?"

Relieved, Jae says, "Oh, Travis, this is Danny Johnston. We dated our sophomore year at NYU."

With a sarcasm-laced tone, I look down at Danny. "You don't say." Jae elbows me slightly… I get the hint. I'm being a dick, but ask me if I care.

Play nice, ok, but I won't like it. Tucking Jae into my side, I ask, "Danny, what do you do?"

Danny narrows his eyes where my hand rests on Jae's hip. Danny isn't stupid… he knows the message that I'm sending. "I stayed in New York after graduating from law school and now work for the Southern District of New York."

"You don't say. Sounds challenging." Leaning in close to Jae, I whisper. "Dance with me." I turn Jae toward the dance floor and call back over my shoulder, "It was nice meeting you, Danny."

Jae isn't happy with me. Knowing Jae, she appreciates the save but not the highhandedness. Watching Danny try to make his move made me want to punch something. I'd seen enough.

"Travis, did you have to be so rude?"

"I didn't like how he was looking at you. Obviously, he wanted a wedding hookup… not on my watch."

"Well, I had him pegged. He asked Vanessa, one of the other bridesmaids, to join him later in his room." Jae shakes her head, then says, "Are you sure that you want to be on the dance floor where you'll be front and center for everyone to see? I don't want you to embarrass yourself."

Leaning down to whisper in Jae's ear, I register the goosebumps that appear. "I'll tell you a secret only Jake and CJ know. Do you remember when I was rehabbing from my soccer injury the summer before going into eleventh grade?"

"Yeah—what about it?"

"The scouts from the colleges started coming to my games. Well, my rehab only got me part of the way back to playing after my tibia surgery. My therapist recommended ballroom dancing." Jacqui chuckles, but

I'm not deterred. "Yeah, I learned how to foxtrot, waltz, salsa, samba. Let's go twinkle toes... prepare to be dazzled."

As I pull Jae into my arms, *What a Wonderful World* by Louis Armstrong plays. Neither one of us says anything, captivated by the moment, lost in our own thoughts. Jae just fits... she feels like the home I always wished I had—warm, welcoming with a cozy fire. I pull her closer to me as we sway and drop a kiss on her shoulder. My body responses immediately. Trying my darnedest to think other thoughts besides how good she feels in my arms. We have to walk back to our table eventually and I don't want to have a raging hard on when we do.

Bending down to her ear, I ask, "How much longer?"

Jae giggles and says, "Eager to leave?" After pausing for a moment, she adds, "I can tell, big guy. Actually, we can leave anytime you're ready, now that all the normal wedding stuff happened."

Stepping back to look at her, my tone playful, I say. "I should warn you I plan to have my wicked way with you."

A deep blush rises in her cheeks, but never one to back down. She says, "You don't say. Do you think we can leave without being too obvious?"

The exit to the large hallway encumbered with a sea of tables... not deterred, I lead Jae off the dance floor. "I'll follow your lead. I need to get you behind closed doors *now*."

"Awwww, you poor deprived baby."

Once Jae grabs her clutch and says her goodbyes, I tuck her in my side and head to the lobby, walking at a fast clip. Once we're in the elevator, I kiss her, trying to convey she's the only girl for me.

Our alma mater made it to the national championship football game. Best part, we lead by two touchdowns at halftime. With everyone occupied with the twins, I seize the opportunity and text Jacqui to meet me down in the wine cellar. As stealth as possible, I head to the wine cellar and anxiously wait for Jacqui to join me.

My heart speeds up when I hear her approach. As soon as she walks into the room, I pull her toward me and whisper, "Took you long enough." Our tongues duel for dominance. My tongue latches onto hers and sucks rhythmically, never wanting to let her go. Needing air, I pull back and drop my forehead to hers while holding her close. "I missed you."

Jae looks equal parts happy to see me and freaked out. "Though I missed you too, we can't stay down here too long. Someone will realize we're both gone."

My groan laced with need as I mumble, "Stay with me tonight." I nibble down Jacqui's neck. "You know you want to."

For better access, I bend my knees to reach the spot behind Jae's ear that drives her out of her mind. "Travis, I... umm... I have nothing to wear to work tomorrow."

Kissing her neck as I continue to state my case, "I'll get up early with you and follow you home. What do you say?"

She pulls back laughing, "Okay, strong argument, counselor. I'll leave a little before the game ends and run by my house to pack a quick bag. Text me when you're heading home and I'll head your way."

My satisfied grin shows how pleased I am with her decision. We both win... I will have Jae in my arms tonight. "Works for me."

With a worried look towards the wine cellar door, Jae bites her lip. "I better head back. See you later, Travis."

"Bye babe."

Reading a work email while I kill time to give Jacqui time to get back to the game, I turn to walk out when Jake appears in the doorway. The surprise shows in my voice. "Heeeeyyyy, Jake." My voice is high pitched even to me.

"So, I figured out a few weeks ago Jacqui was seeing someone new and assumed she just hadn't gotten around to telling me yet."

Before Jake continues, I interrupt him. "Jake, look I... this... this started innocently enough. She needed a plus one for Brittney's wedding. Over these past two months, I've gotten to know Jacqui."

In disbelief, Jake looks at me keenly. "But you... you have always been allergic to relationships."

"My primary goal was being there for Jacqui, especially after the nightmare engagement with Jeremy." I look down, trying to collect my thoughts. Debating if I should come all the way clean with Jake.

Jake studies me like he studies an architectural design issue. Before I can continue talking, Jake jumps in. "You're in love with her. Aren't you?"

I swallow the golf ball size lump in my throat and hang my head. "Yeah, I am."

Jake paces. "I love you like a brother, man. If I'm being honest, I can't say that I would have picked you for Jacqui."

I wince because I get it. If I had a little sister, I wouldn't pick me either. "I need you to know that I would never hurt Jacqui. I'm just coming to terms with this myself, but I've loved Jacqui since our junior year of high school."

Incredulously, Jake looks like he wants to strangle me. "Shit, Travis. Are you kidding me? Really! Since high school? But why didn't you say anything before now?"

"Believe me, I tried not to think of her. I knew she was off limits." I hang my head and say defeatedly, "No one, and I mean no one, has ever come close to Jacqui. She's the standard. I compare *everyone* to her." I look Jake in the eye and say earnestly, "Everyone."

Jake looks at me like he's seeing me for the first time. "Does she know?"

"No, I'm so far out of my element right now. The only thing that I've come up with is to take it one day at a time and just be there for her."

"I don't want to see her hurt again. Jeremy did a real number on her." He continues to pace again as he runs his hand across the back of his neck. My gaze laser focused as Jake walks back and forth. "Being a twin, Jacqui and I have a unique relationship different from other siblings, but I promise not to intervene. Seeing her smile again makes me happy for her. I love seeing the light back in her eyes."

Relieved Jake takes pity on me. "Any advice?"

"Don't fuck this up." I groan… not helpful AT ALL. "All kidding aside, be open and honest with her. You'll know the right time to tell her how you feel."

"Thanks man. This means a lot."

Chapter Twelve

C hapter Twelve

Jacqui

After speaking with Travis earlier, I decide to surprise him with lunch from our favorite Thai restaurant. The Pad Thai contains the perfect balance of lime and heat for me. Travis prefers the lemongrass on a bed of lettuce for him since his triathlon occurs in less than six weeks.

After exiting the elevator, I notice his secretary isn't at her desk, so I turn the corner to his office and stop in my tracks. Travis holds a woman I don't know in an embrace. I see the woman turn her head as she reaches for a kiss.

Slapped with the reality of another man's infidelity... when will I ever learn? Shocked, I stand frozen in the doorway. Shaking my head as I slowly back out of his office, I drop the lunch and run blindly to the elevator. The elevator opened, giving me an opportunity to jump in with seconds to spare. As the door closes, Travis stands about three feet away with a pained expression.

Shit, the elevator contains at least four people who watched my life crumble right before my eyes. A tear drops, but I refuse to cry in front of these strangers. Can't this thing go any faster? Finally, we arrive in the lobby. My car sits a few spots in the front. With tears streaming down my face, I start the car, reverse and drive.

As I'm driving off, I see an out of breath Travis in my review mirror. My phone rings. I decline. I don't want to hear his lies. Jeremy told one lie after another... *she means nothing to me. You're the one that I want. Remember, I asked you to marry me, not her.* When these excuses didn't work, he went for my insecurities... *if you were more attentive, I would have never looked for comfort in another woman's arms. If you filled my needs in bed, no way I would have ever looked at another woman. You could have prevented us from reaching this point if you had given me more attention rather than being preoccupied with the wedding.* Driving straight home, I call my office and let them know that I'll be out for the rest of the afternoon.

Walking into the kitchen to drop my purse and laptop on the table, memories of Travis and me making love on the counter replay in vivid detail. How did I let down my guard? Not my smartest move to fall for the consummate king of one-night stands. What the hell was I thinking? Travis, holding that woman, flashes on a constant loop. Something deep breaks within me as I climb into bed. I wail with heart-wrenching sobs until I have nothing left.

The next morning, still unable to face anyone, I call in sick and head back to bed as I look down at my phone - thirty missed calls from Travis. Flipping my phone over on my nightstand, I pull the covers over my head and try to go back to sleep.

Sleep evades me. Every time I close my eyes... I see Travis with that woman. Travis always was a player. Momma G says a leopard never changes its spots. Why did I let myself believe he changed? Once a player, always a player. I should have known better.

Day three, I haven't washed my hair and now sit in my bed with a pint of Ben & Jerry's Chocolatey Love A-Fair watching *Fault in our Stars*. My front door chime beeps. Wonder what took him so long. After a minute,

Jake stands in my bedroom door, taking an assessment of the mess in front of him. When he notices my go-to-cry-my-eyes-out movie on my TV, he slowly walks into my room and sits on my bed.

"Is this about Travis?"

What? He knew? Since when? Jake knows me better than anyone. When we were around four, one of our classmates, Jimmy, told me I was ugly and that I smelled like a girl. Jake walked over to Jimmy, punched him in the nose and dared Jimmy to say it again. Jake always has my back. We called ourselves the *wonder twins*. Well, here goes nothing. "How? How did you know?"

"I just recently discovered you were seeing each other."

"Yeah, well, it's over."

He slides his eyes to me and asks, "Are you sure?"

"Yes, I'm sure. Travis had another woman in his arms when I walked into his office. I've already had to deal with Jeremy's infidelity. I need to end this before I... before I." I crumble and start crying. My feelings for Travis are deep... my heart breaks all over again.

Jake pulls me into his arms, "Oh Jae." He holds me until I finally stop crying. "Do you want to talk about it?"

Mumbling against his chest, I refuse to look up. "I don't know. Are you mad I didn't tell you I was seeing Travis?"

Jake continues to hold me. "No Jae. At first, I just guessed you were seeing someone. It wasn't until the night of the Texas championship win where I put everything together." He pauses. "Look, I need you to know that I'm always Team Jacqui. No matter what. You can talk to me. Would it help if I punch him in the nose like I did Jimmy?"

With a watery laugh, I continue to hug Jake as tears flow. Finally finding the courage, I lean against my pillows and tell Jake what happened. "I went to surprise Travis for lunch on Monday only to come face to face with Travis having a woman in his arms who was getting ready to kiss him. We both know Travis is the consummate bachelor. I'm more pissed at myself. I should have known better."

Jake nods his agreement. He scans my tear-stained face and takes a pause before asking, "If Gabi and I hadn't had our misunderstanding, I probably wouldn't ask, but are you sure you know what you walked in on?"

With a sarcastic huff, I wrap my arms around myself to hold it together. "Not much to misunderstand. He had a woman wrapped in his arms. End of story."

"I'm not taking his side, Jae. Just asking. What do you need? I see you already have your favorite ice cream and movie. Would you like me to stay a bit? I've already watched the movie with you more times than I can count, but I'm here for you."

"Jake, I'll be okay. Just need time to lick my wounds. Go home to your girls."

Travis

Driving around mindlessly for the past hour damn near on autopilot when I notice I'm nearing Jake's house. I hang my head... how did I end up here? Here goes nothing... desperate times after all. Another point of view would help. I have tried calling Jacqui over fifty times and stopped by her house a few times, but she refuses to answer either.

The front door opens as I approach. Jake opens the door and says, "I've been expecting you. Gabi knows you're here. Let's head down to the humidor. I was going to recommend a beer, but after taking one look at you, you look like you need a bourbon."

We walk in silence until he closes the door to the humidor. After learning that they were expecting, Jake redesigned this room with a separate ventilation system. Sinking into one of the soft brown leather chairs that overlook the pool and patio in the backyard, I accept the two-finger pour of bourbon. Mesmerized by the amber liquid, like maybe the answers will magically appear.

Jake silently watches me for a few minutes then asks, "Do you want to talk about it?"

"I drove for the past hour without a clear destination. Maybe subconsciously, I knew I needed to talk to you. Do you know what happened?"

"A little, but I'd love to hear your side."

I looked shocked for a moment... surprised Jake wasn't kicking my ass right now after making Jacqui cry. The one thing I promised not to do. I clear my throat. "Gwen stopped by my office. She said she needed advice on her dad's estate. Her dad passed away suddenly from a heart attack last year. When she started crying, I gave her a shoulder to cry on. I swear that was it. Gwen misinterpreted my support. She stood on her tiptoes and tried to kiss me."

My head drops and my voice goes softer. "This is when Jacqui walked into my office. It looked bad, but I swear nothing happened. Needing to explain to Jacqui, I ran after her. She made it to her car and was driving away by the time I ran down ten flights of stairs." My voice cracks, "I can't lose her, man. I can't."

Jake stares into bourbon glass absorbing everything I've said. "Kicking you while you're down won't do you any good right now. We'll talk later about strategies I have put in place to make sure women know I'm happily married and not in the market for any extracurricular activities. For now, don't give up. Try calling her in the morning and, for good measure, call from the front of her house."

Almost feeling like this is my punishment, my penance would be losing Jae. I need Jake to provide more guidance. My gut tells me I only get one shot. "What do I say? After the shit that Jeremy put her through, I know she has trust issues. I swear on my nonno's grave that nothing happened. Jacqui is it for me. I only want her."

"Speak from your heart. Tell her what you shared with me, but more. She needs to know you feel. Make sure she knows that you're not just killing time."

Hope dares to take root. I need to find a way to make her believe.

Despite only getting two hours of sleep, I lay wide awake in bed at six in the morning. Swinging my legs over the bed, I put my head in my hands and groan. Everything hurts. I feel like I have been in a UFC fight where I lost. Hopefully, a shower and a strong cup of coffee will do the trick.

The shower helped to remove some of the stress held in my shoulders. Replaying Jake's advice helps me prepare what I want to say to Jae. Pulling a long sleeve gray Henley and blue jeans as I get ready, I walk to the kitchen for a much-needed cup of coffee. The tremble in my hands signifies even my body knows... my future hangs in the balance. Everything hinges on her agreement to see me today.

My pulse pounds rapidly as I look down at my watch and notice four hours passed while I sat in my study. Visions of Jacqui smiling at me flood my memories. I send a silent prayer that she will at least listen to me as I grab my keys from the counter and head to Jacqui's house.

Fifteen minutes later, I park and dial Jacqui's number as I lean my head against the headrest. Ready for my call to go to voicemail as it has every day this week. I sit rod straight when I hear Jacqui answer.

The tentative voice on the other side of the line confirms I need to lay my feelings bare at her feet if I want even a slight chance at winning her back. "Hi Travis."

Before answering, I clear my throat to settle my nerves. "Jae, can I come in?"

Muffled shuffling sounds come through the phone. "You're here?"

Opening my car door, I stand so she can see me. When I see the door open, I release the breath I am holding and walk up the sidewalk. Jacqui puts her hand in the middle of my chest, stopping me from walking inside. "You have ten minutes."

Damn, okay, I can do this. I extend my arm toward her living room. "Can we sit?" She nods her head and walks to the couch with her arms wrapped around her for protection. My eyes greedily search her every feature... eyes appear to be slightly puffy and her nose is a little red. My heart feels like a knife has been driven through my chest knowing I'm the cause of her hurt. Only wanting to love her never hurt her. Conviction boils in my veins... I will fix this.

"Jae, I know how it looked, but I swear to you nothing happened. Over this week, I have looked at the situation through your eyes and I want to say that I understand. I also take responsibility for putting myself in a compromising position. I should have known better. Gwen flirted with me in the past, but I never gave her a sign that I was interested. She saw an opening and tried to capitalize on an opportunity that she misinterpreted was there. Can you ever forgive me? Can give me another chance?"

She eyes me with disbelief but continues to sit next to me. "I don't know Travis. You're asking for a lot."

Holding her hands in mine, I feel the apprehension permeating from her and sense she's pulling away. Losing Jae would level me. I'd never recover. My voice cracks as I look earnestly into her eyes, "Jacqui, I should have told you sooner, but I love you. I really love you. You knocked me on my ass. I never believed I could love, but I know I love you."

Jae eyes me suspiciously, not buying what I'm selling. "How do you know Travis?"

"This is what I know, without a doubt. One, you and I click. I've never laughed as much as I do with you. Two, even after spending time with you, I can't wait to see you again. Three, you are the first person I want to talk to when I wake in the morning and the last person at night. Four, your smile makes my day. I mean, everything could go wrong and I still would have a great day because you are in it. Five, I love sharing my space with you. I love seeing your makeup, perfume, and clothes next to mine." I pause, giving Jacqui time to process everything that I've shared. "What do you say, Jae? Can you give me another chance? I promise not to do a boneheaded thing like that again."

A lone tear drops, then another. I use my thumb to wipe them away and pray she will give us another chance.

She smiles as she says, "You were boneheaded."

"No arguments from me. What do you say about us making this relationship official? I really want to take you on another date."

Jacqui takes a shuttered breath. She's thinking so hard right now, I swear I can hear her thoughts. Her hands in mine, I say, "Babe, I know that my reputation precedes me. You have my word. You never have to worry about me betraying your trust. I only want you."

Trying to be patient and give Jae time, I pause. Right when I'm ready to give my third closing argument, Jacqui takes pity on me, leans over, and gives me a tender kiss that rocks me to my core.

Jacqui

Saying I have trust issues is an understatement... my trust issues have trust issues. At first, I wanted to say no, but then I realized I was punishing Travis for Jeremy's wrongdoings. I can't do that to him. I love him too much. Shaken, I almost closed down the possibility of being with Travis and ever knowing he loved me.

"Travis, I love you too. I should probably send Jeremy and his fiancée a wedding gift. Without them, I wouldn't have found you." before continuing, not sure how Travis will react, I hesitate. "I want us to date openly, so you know what that means."

"Yeah, I do. You want your mom and dad to know about us? No arguments from me. Attending our gatherings together is what I want. Having to drive separately and pretend I couldn't care less where you were going. Every time you left, I always worried something could happen while you were in transit."

Leaning over, I kiss him softly before saying, "I love seeing your sweet side. Knowing how difficult it is for you to let others into your life means the world to me you let me in." Enough talk. My need for Travis is intense. As I kiss Travis on his neck and nibble his ear, I whisper, "Take me to bed."

He gathers me in his lap and stands with me in his arms as he says, "Jae, I love you so much."

Travis lays me down and begins pulling down my yoga pants. Lifting, I remove my top and begin helping Travis with his shirt. Both of our hands land at the top of his sweats. The tent in his sweats makes my mouth water. I need him now. Not waiting, I dip my hands, grab his hard cock and pump his silky rod.

Our eagerness builds. Travis pulls down his sweats, grabs a condom from the nightstand, and drops his head as he rolls on the condom. Plunging into me with perfect precision... filling me completely as we move with desperation, realizing how close to losing each other we came. No longer having to hold back, I freely say the words that fill my heart, "I love you, Travis."

My climax builds as Travis hits my clit with each long stroke going deeper and deeper. Gripping his shoulders, I move with him in our special rhythm.

Travis

Making love to Jae keeps me grounded, but barely. I pour my soul into every stroke, making love to my Jacqui. "Baby, I love you... I love you so very much."

Jae tightens her grip on my cock in a rhythm that is driving me out of my mind. "Travis, I feel your love. I'm close, but I don't want to come yet. I want this to last. You feel so good."

"Jae, I'm going to make love to you all night. Don't hold back. Come now... come now for me."

I reach between us and work her clit, using my calloused thumb. Jae tightens around me. Oh, God... her climax comes quick and hard, triggering mine. Losing the battle to keep my movements smooth, my climax goes on and on. Having Jacqui back in my arms, a sense of peace flows over me. With Jae in my arms, a reality hits me... my stupid, innocent mistake almost cost me the love of my life.

We struggle to catch our breath. Jacqui looks so beautiful to me, even with eyes puffy from crying. I bend and kiss her, emotionally rocked to be the one that Jae chose. "Love you, Jae."

"Love you, Travis."

Epilogue

Six Months Later
Jacqui

"Travis, you know you are setting the bar high, don't you?" We have a suite at the Hotel Plaza Athenee in Paris overlooking the Eiffel Tower to celebrate our six-month dating anniversary. These six months have been a dream. True to his word, Travis showers me with love every day.

My favorites are the *'just because'* surprises. After a long day, Travis gives me a foot massage or he'll make my favorite smoothie for breakfast when I have a hectic morning. We split our time between each of our houses, but find that we stay at mine more since I have several commissions underway that I'm painting.

Finally garnering the courage to tell my dad I did not want to be the next chief operations officer; the conversation was hard, but my dad listened. Shocked best describes my dad's response. He knew I dabbled in painting, but shared he considered it a hobby. When I revealed how much I'd made from my paintings in the past six months, pride and amazement glowed on his face. We ended the discussion with dad giving me his support as I decide my timing to transition full-time to painting.

Walking into the living room after his shower, I pause... amazed that he's mine. Knowing how much I love his five o'clock shadow, he finds any excuse to indulge me. Before I register my movement, I walk over and meet him halfway. "Hey, handsome."

"Hey, yourself. Our dinner should arrive any minute." On cue, the doorbell to our suite rings.

The bellman enters the room and removes the covers to each of the entrees as he sets them on the dining table. Our dinner smells delicious, so far so good, not feeling nauseous.

Before we left for Paris, my doctor's office called with the results from my tests and confirmed I did not have a stomach bug. The nurse informed me the test was positive. She couldn't confirm my exact due date but helped me find an appointment in the next two weeks to pinpoint the date.

We started talking about kids a few months ago after babysitting the twins for Jake and Gabi so they could go on a much-needed date night. Travis shared his concerns about whether he could be a good father, but confided he really wants us to have kids. I mostly listened but shared my observations of his character and all the love he freely gives to our family circle. I plan to tell him tonight. The perfect time will present itself.

While we eat our meal, we discuss our favorite art from yesterday's visit to the Louvre as Nat King Cole's *Mona Lisa* plays in the background. No surprise, Travis loved the Mona Lisa.

The Louvre remains my favorite museum. My NYU art professor helped me secure tickets for a closed exhibit after I asked for his help. Seeing additional paintings by Van Gogh, Picasso, and Monet, normally not on display, filled me with awe and inspiration.

Lost in thought, admiring the beauty of the Eiffel Tower, I turn and notice Travis on one knee. Surprised, I gasp and place my hands over my mouth. Oh my God! This is happening.

Travis opens the engagement ring in the Tiffany box. My focus only on Travis. "Jacqui, I have loved you since I was seventeen. I want to spend the rest of my life with you, growing old together with kids filling our house. I'd love a boy and a girl, but I don't mind being a girl dad either. Know that I'm always in your corner and your biggest cheerleader. Would you make me the happiest man in the world and say yes to being my wife? Jacqui, will you marry me?"

I'm a mess, crying, laughing and nodding my head. "Yes, Travis. Yes, I will marry you." I feel him slip the ring on my finger as we both rise. I bury my head in his neck and feel cherished in his arms.

"Um, Travis, I have something that I need to tell you. You may want to sit down for this."

Travis senses the seriousness in my voice and sits. "What is it?"

"I've been trying to tell you since I got the news and planned to tell you after dessert. Do you remember when I had that really severe sinus infection a little over a month ago?"

Travis nods but remains quiet. "Yeah, and for the past two weeks, you have had some sort of stomach flu."

"After you threatened to carry me to the doctor if that's what it took, I went to the doctor earlier this week. I don't have a stomach flu. Well, here's the deal." I take a fortifying breath before I continue. "You are going to get your wish of starting a family… probably sooner than you wanted."

Travis

Standing, I lift Jacqui and squeeze her gently. "Baby, I can't believe it. When I thought I had lost you, I resigned myself that I'd be alone for the rest of my life. I believed this was just another way that I was being punished for even daring to exist in this world." I give her a kiss, pouring my love and gratitude for the gift of having her in my life. "Jacqui, you have made me the happiest man in the world! I want to shout to any and everybody 'She chose me! And she's *HAVING* MY BABY.' I love you, Jae. Love you with all of my heart."

She grabs my face and kisses me again. "I love you Travis so much."

When she pulls back, the inquisitive expression on her faces gives me a clue that I need to brace for the next question. "How did dad take the news? How did Jake take the news?"

About a month ago, I went to visit Jacqui's father. I found him in his garage tinkering with his vintage 1957 baby blue and white corvette. I handed him a glass of cold, iced sweet tea. When I cleared my throat, he sensed this was going to be a serious talk.

He leaned against the car and said, "What is it, son?" I had an entire speech ready, but all that came out was, "Papa Mac, I know I probably wouldn't be your first choice for Jacqui, but I love her sir and I want to marry her. I hope I have your blessing."

When he responded, "Son, this is where you are wrong." My heart dropped. I knew the chances of him blessing our union was a long shot, but then he continued, "I secretly wished you and Jacqui would end up together. Christine and I give our blessing. You are already part of our family, son. This just makes it official." I gave him a big hug, trying not to spill our drinks.

Now Jake, he couldn't let the opportunity to tease me pass. His teasing sounded similar to the ribbing that I gave him. He said, "Gabi and I bet you were going to ask Jacqui to marry you on Valentine's Day." When I rub the back of my neck, he laughed and said, "I knew it."

After pausing, I start, "I probably shouldn't arm you with this ammunition. I purchased the ring before Valentine's Day and have been waiting for the right time. Man, I know keeping the relationship secret wasn't cool, but I thank you for having my back in the end."

Jake grabbed my shoulder. "You have more than shown how much you love my sister. Any doubts that I had in the beginning are gone. I've always considered you a brother, and soon it will be official." I got choked up. Gave him a man clap on the back and said, "Love you, man."

My smile broadens on my face. "Jacqui, when I spoke to your dad, I was nervous like the first time I had to give a presentation at a global board meeting. Your dad, always astute, knew something was up. He listened to me stumbling over asking for his blessing and immediately put me out of my misery."

I continue, "Now Jake, he couldn't help but tease me about how hard I fell. Unfortunately, I'm not ashamed to say that I teased him about Gabi and wanting to ask her to marry him when he had just met her during our seven-day cruise."

I sit back down. Looking up at her, "Can I see?" At first, she's confused, then realizes I want to see the baby bump. She slowly lifts her shirt. Reverently touching her stomach, I whisper, "Oh, I see a slight bump here, our baby." I lean forward and kiss her stomach. "Hey baby, this is your daddy." I stand before the woman that I love more than life itself. "How are you feeling now?"

"Feeling a little better. The waves of nausea come and go, but nothing like before."

"You've made me the happiest man in the world, but I hate knowing I'm the reason you've been sick." Pausing before continuing, I say, "I love you, Jae. I plan to make you happy." I just realized she will probably start showing soon. "Do you know how long you want our engagement to be?"

"Since I was little, I always dreamed of a big wedding. Now all I want is something intimate with our family and close friends. If it's alright with you, I'd rather not look like a beached whale in the wedding pictures.

Any concerns if we have a summer wedding in about two months in my parents' backyard?"

"Baby, I'd marry you at a truck stop if that was your dream wedding. I love the idea of getting married at your parents' house. Now that's settled, I want to take my fiancée to bed and make love to her all night long."

"I'm all yours."

Also By

A Love Blossoms Series Novel
Could This Be Love (Gabi and Jake), Book #1

For You to Love (Gabi and Jake), Book #2

My Fake Holiday Love (Jacqui and Travis), Book #3
Next Book in Series
Samantha and CJ, Book #4

About the Author

ABOUT THE AUTHOR

CD Giles

Living in the Texas Hill Country with her husband of nearly twenty years, CD Giles is a romantic at heart. Her storybook reunion with her sweetheart began in junior high school. After twenty-two years of bad timing and missed opportunities, the stars finally aligned during a group trip together as adults. They've been together ever since their official first date. C.D. loves a good happily-ever-after story--after all, she's living one! When she's not penning one herself, she's watching rom-coms and spending time with family.

Website: https://www.cdgiles.com

Instagram: https://instagram.com/cdgilesauthor/

www.ingramcontent.com/pod-product-compliance
Lightning Source LLC
Chambersburg PA
CBHW020548160726
47991CB00002B/643